You're

ISBN   Softcover   978-0-6451512-8-2
         eBook   978-0-6451512-7-5

Published by: Reading Stones Publishing
Helen Brown & Wendy Wood
Woodwendy1982.wixsite.com/readingstones

Cover Design: Wendy Wood
Cover Photo: Wendy Wood
Cover Photo is of a church in Leyburn, Queensland, Australia

For more copies contact the author at:

Glenburnie Homestead
212 Glenburnie Road
ROB ROY NSW 2360
Mobile: 0422 577 663
Email: readingstonespublishing@gmail.com

You're

Healing Broken Hearts in Huntersville

Helen Brown

Reading Stones Publishing

Trigger Warning

This book deals with issues surrounding Domestic Violence. Including descriptions of abuse, violence and its impacts and injuries.

It is hoped that people would be encouraged to understand what it is, and that there is always hope for a recovery, even if it takes much longer than expressed in these stories.

If this book raises issues for you, please seek help and support in your local area.

Disclaimer:

This book is a work of fiction, while the stories were inspired by real situations, any reference to any actual person or event is entirely coincidental.

Acknowledgement

The Story titled *Casey*, was originally written as *'Casey's New Life'* for Power of Change's Short Story competition in 2022.

It inspired the rest of the stories that comprise this volume.

The original story can be found in the short story collection published at: www.powertochange.org.au

Contents

Susan

Susan curled up on her bed and sobbed a flood of tears. Her marriage to Michael was nothing like what she imagined it would be. She had read some magazines that had given her some romantic notions, but her reality turned out to be something completely different, even on her wedding night.

Michael hadn't even tried to be gentle with her and when the tears had flowed, his impatience had been so hurtful. She had struggled through their honeymoon, which seemed to lack any sweetness and left her thinking that it was a strange name for something that was so bitter.

Each day had been wrought with problems. She tried to work out what she could do to make him happy, but it just seemed to be impossible. If she wanted to stay in bed, he got mad, so the next day she got up early and he still got cranky. It seemed that she couldn't do a thing right.

Once they had returned home, they had visited her parents and she had tried to talk to her mother by herself in the kitchen, but her mother had simply told her to "suck it up" and get on with making her husband happy. When she had asked her mother how she was supposed to do that, her reply was that she should figure it out by herself.

Over the last two years, things hadn't improved. Michael had even stopped hitting her where the bruises couldn't be seen. When they went out to dinner, he would explain them away as her being a clumsy, ditsy, female, a story that most of his business associates seemed to buy.

Over the years, she had a broken arm and a couple of ribs. During the stay in hospital, having miscarried her baby after another session of Michael's *correction* of her behaviour, she'd overheard a nurse talking to a colleague just outside her room, they apparently thought she was asleep.

'She'll end up in the morgue, that one. I've seen this so many times before and it's one of the reasons that I have decided to only be married to my career.'

Then last night, when they had been at a party, after Michael had left a cut on her eyebrow that required stitches, his solicitor had made a comment about how she should be more careful and she had replied, 'I wish I could command angels to guard me from my clumsiness.' He had laughed quietly, but Michael's face had looked like thunder. How she didn't have any broken bones this time was a miracle, maybe God's angels had been there after all. Not only had he given her a beating last night, but he had continued this morning. There was no point talking to her parents, they had told her so many times that it was her fault that she couldn't make her husband happy.

His parents just never seemed to like her either. His mother, in particular, would pick on every little thing that she did. Thank goodness she hadn't got pregnant again.

'God, I can't take this anymore. Hell cannot be as hard as this. Sorry, God, please forgive me'. She got up, dressing in the same pencil skirt and jacket outfit that she had worn while shopping the day before. Michael had insisted the new fashion of flared skirts would be inappropriate for a woman married to a man of his standing in society. Going to the kitchen, she stoked up the firebox. Without checking that she had secured the door properly, she walked out of the house and made her way to the river.

She stood there, just for a minute looking at the murky water, and jumped.

The water was much colder than she expected, taking her breath away and the current underneath the smooth surface was a lot stronger than she anticipated. Suddenly she wanted to live, as long as she didn't have to be anywhere near Michael. *Relax.* Someone was talking to her. As she did, she broke the surface of the water and discovered that the current had already carried her around the bend of the river out of sight of the neighbourhood. *Roll over, float, and let the water take you to safety.*

As she floated down the river, she was surprised that no-one seemed to see her. Just as dusk was starting to fall, she bumped into the bank. She closed her eyes. She figured that if she slept here all night, she would be able to get up in the morning and walk away, to where, she had no idea.

'Oh, come on, let me help you out of there.'

She opened her eyes and found herself looking into the kind face of a man. Slowly she realised that she recognised this man, he had been sitting on a bench in the street and witnessed Michael dragging her into their car the day before.

'Please don't tell anyone I'm here', she pleaded. 'I can't go back. Please!!' He gently lifted her out of the water and carried her, as if she was a small child, back to his house.

'Please, don't tell anyone about what I did', she'd cried to the man's wife who had taken her into a small bedroom. As she helped her out of her clothes, an involuntary gasp escaped her.

'You have a husband?'

'Please don't report me, I doubt he will let me run away again.'

'It's alright dear, I was a nurse before I married my husband. Thankfully he is the kindest man and has never raised his hand to me or our child. I saw a lot of women like you while I was working.'

'I know what I have done is unforgivable, but I would rather live like Cain than go home.'

'I would consider what your husband has done to be unforgivable. Don't worry, you will be safe here for a little while as we have very few visitors. What's your name?'

'Susan Joanne Landtry.'

'From Mount Grandsville?' Susan nodded. 'Which name are you known by?'

'Susan.'

'Well, around here we will call you Jo. A new name for a new start. There's not much to you, it's a miracle you made it this far.'

She wrapped her up in a blanket, led her back into the kitchen and made her sit beside the fire which her husband had stoked up while they were out of the room. The farmer had made a pot of tea and poured it into three large, enamelled mugs. He quietly handed her a cup into which he had stirred two spoons of sugar.

'I'd better finish milking the cows, they won't do it themselves.' He smiled at his wife, kissed her cheek, and walked out of the house.

After she had drunk the tea and eaten some toast with cheese, the farmer's wife bathed her cuts and bruises with salted water and insisted that she go and get some sleep.

When she woke in the morning the sun was shining through the window. It took her a minute to work out where she was. As she looked around her, memories of the previous day flooded in but so did the feeling that she was finally safe from Michael's *lessons*. She climbed out of bed, finding that her clothes had been washed, dried, and placed over the chair in the corner.

She dressed slowly because her cuts and bruises made movement very hard. There was a quiet knock on her door and the farmer's wife entered without asking if she was decent.

'I thought I heard you get up; I want to bathe those cuts again before you finish getting dressed.' The cuts stung as the salt water was applied but not as bad as they had the night before.

When they entered the kitchen, breakfast was laid out and her saviour was hoeing into a large plate of bacon, eggs, sausages, and toast. A plate containing bacon and eggs was placed in front of her and she suddenly felt very hungry.

'I hope you don't mind, but my husband and I have been talking about your situation. My sister has recently lost her husband and lives on a farm near a small town, considered by many to be in the middle of nowhere. I'm going to visit her tomorrow by train, so we think that it might be good for you to come with me, and if my sister is agreeable, you could stay with her and help her on the farm. It will be hard work, but it probably will be the last place for someone to go looking for you. I found some of my son's work clothes so, if you put them on, and we hide your hair, no-one will look twice at a mother and son travelling together.'

Susan looked from one to the other in amazement. 'You'd do that for me?'

'Yes,' said the farmer, 'as my wife said, it's not right what has been done to you. I believe that God would have a hard time forgiving us if we allowed you to go back to your husband.'

'But what if your sister doesn't want me to stay at her place?'

'We'll worry about that if it happens, right now, it's more important to get you as far away from here as possible. I think this is God's way of guarding your life.' Susan looked at the lady, *was she right? Were these people God's angels that He had sent to guard her?*

Missus Brown, as Susan now knew her, packed some of her son's clothes. 'It's not much, but at least it will give you something to start with.' And the next evening they found themselves being dropped off at the railway station by Mister Brown. He purchased their tickets and a newspaper for them to read on the journey. Having installed them in the carriage, he kissed his wife's cheek and shook Susan's hand, saying 'May the Lord go with you.' He left the carriage and the train pulled out. They had deliberately chosen the night train in the hope that very few people would try to make conversation with them.

There was sufficient light to start reading the newspaper. As Susan unfolded it, a headline jumped out at her, she gasped.

'What is it, dear?'

Susan handed the newspaper to her. There on the front page was a photo of her house, burnt to the ground.

'I must have forgotten to close the door on the stove securely,' she said in a whisper. 'He'll have to go back and live with his parents now I suspect. Serves him right. That's the one thing we had in common, he couldn't do anything right in their eyes either. I'm pretty sure that's the reason he got married, to get away from them.'

They read the story, it mentioned that, because of the unsafe state of the house, a thorough investigation had not yet been carried out but at this stage, it was presumed that Susan Landtry, the owner's wife, had perished in the fire.

'Well at least they won't be looking for you for a little while.'

'Yes, thank goodness.'

They continued their journey in silence, dozing off as best as they could in the hard seats.

It was late afternoon by the time they reached their destination. Missus Brown's sister was waiting on the platform when the train pulled in. 'Just stay back for a bit will you please, while I explain things to her.'

Missus Brown hugged her sister, and Susan watched as they had a short conversation. Missus Brown turned around and indicated that Susan should join them. 'This is my sister Elsa, Elsa, this is Susan, but we've decided to call her by her middle name, Jo.'

'There's not much to her, I hope she can do her fair share of the work.'

'Well, you will have to show me what to do, I've never worked on a farm before.'

'I'll give you a go, if you can keep house, that will at least help me keep up with the outside work. Come on then, time is a-wasting.'

They bundled into a farm ute and drove out of town on a road that Susan thought could only be considered to be not much more than a bush track.

On their arrival at the farm, Elsa showed Susan her room, which turned out to be an attachment to the outside of the house. She looked around and breathed a sigh of relief. She should be safe here. 'Thank you, God, for this second chance. I promise to pay you back by helping others who find themselves in the same position.'

During the first week of Missus Brown's stay, Susan insisted that she learn as much as she could about farming life. After day three, Susan found that she was able to get up just as early as the other members of the household. When it was time for Missus Brown to return home, Susan stayed on the farm. She promised Elsa that if anyone came visiting, she would stay hidden under the bed in her room. She hugged Missus Brown and thanked her for everything she had done. The sisters promised to write and report any news without letting on that Susan was there.

With the clean air, no stress, and plenty of sleep, it wasn't long before Susan was able to not only have breakfast ready, but most of the housework done by the time Elsa returned from milking the cows. She worked hard and started to help Elsa outside as well. She also discovered that she really enjoyed cooking, now that Michael wasn't complaining about everything that she made. She was surprised to discover that those who visited relished her cakes and sweets.

Things rolled along very nicely for a few months. Elsa and Susan became good friends, something Susan wouldn't have thought possible the day she arrived. Then one day, Elsa had a fall while she was out in the paddock. Susan was able to get her into the Ute and drive her into the township to see the doctor.

It appeared that her leg was broken, and the doctor was doubtful that she would be able to carry on farming for much longer. That night, Susan, having fed the animals and milked the cows, sat beside her friend as she was resting.

'What do we do now?'

'I think it's time to sell the farm. I have two neighbours who have been sniffing around since Terry died. Tomorrow, after the chores are done, I'd like you to go and visit them and ask them to come and see me. I want them both here at the same time and you are to be my witness.'

'But what will you do after that? Where will you live? And where will I go?'

'Don't panic, Jo.' Susan smiled, she had never been able to call herself by her middle name, not that it seemed to matter out here in the middle of nowhere. People just accepted that she was working alongside Elsa, just as Elsa had worked beside her husband while he was alive, they had long ago dropped the pretence that she was a boy. The most contact they had with people was at the monthly church service as they entertained very few visitors.

'How would you feel about making a living out of your cooking?' Elsa's question broke into her thoughts.

'Do you think I could?'

'Well, you mightn't make a fortune, but I know that there's a building in the main street that could be used for such a purpose. There's also a house in Church Street that is up for sale. If I get enough out of the sale of the farm, I would like to buy both buildings and set up a tearoom business, it should make us enough to live on. What do you think?'

'Oh, Elsa, that would be wonderful. I can't believe how good God has been to me.'

It turned out that the neighbours were not only very competitive, but also very determined to add Elsa's property to their portfolios. The price she was able to obtain surprised even Elsa. It took a few weeks, but the sale of the farm and purchase of the two buildings in town went through.

Susan made a conscious decision to work in the back of the shop, leaving Elsa to take care of the customers. This way she didn't have to deal with the public, reducing the risk of accidently meeting someone who might have known her in her old life.

Now that they were living in town, they received their mail and newspaper more regularly. One day, they received a letter from Elsa's sister to say that her husband had witnessed a car accident the night before, in which it appeared that Susan's husband and his parents had been killed. Later, as she was reading the paper, she came across a death notice for Michael Landtry and his parents. 'Well, I'll be dammed!' said Elsa.

Three weeks later she was reading the latest issue of the paper when she came across a notice placed by the Landtry's solicitor. It was headed *IMPORTANT*. "Would Jo Landtry, the last surviving relative of Michael, Henry, and Pauline Landtry, contact my office in writing. Please mark correspondence *Private Confidential*.

'Elsa, what should I do? This could be someone's trick to get me to pay for burning down my house?'

'The decision is yours, but you know that God has protected you to this point in time, so pray about it. He may have a good reason for contacting you, the solicitor, I mean. It won't necessarily be bad news.'

She sat down and stared at the note paper in front of her. What should she write? How did he know that she was going to use the name Jo? Were the police after her for burning down the house? She thought back over the months since she'd arrived in Huntersville and how God had taken care of her, so she put pen to paper, but all she wrote was the address of the bakery, and Luke 4:10.

Two weeks later, Elsa showed Mister Henderson into the kitchen of the shop.

'Susan, it's so good to see you so well.'

'Am I in trouble?'

'No, Michael never got around to changing his will which means that, as the only surviving member of the family, there is a considerable fortune for you to inherit.'

'But I'm supposed to be dead.'

'There are legal ways around that, leave those details to me. What would you like me to do with the assets?'

'I've been thinking about something a lot over the time I've been here actually. I've been trying to figure out how to make it happen. I would like to set up a trust to assist those who find themselves in similar circumstances to the one I found myself in after my marriage to Michael.'

'What a good idea, I'm sorry I didn't have the courage to try and do anything to help. The family was very powerful.'

'Society needs to change its collective attitude towards women before anything real can happen. I pray that, one day, it will be considered a crime equal to those against men. In the meantime, I promised God, when He saved my life, that I would pay Him back by helping those who are struggling with the same problem.'

I'm sure that God loves you and isn't expecting you to keep that promise.'

'I know that, but I cannot stand by and do nothing when He has done so much for me.' Mister Henderson raised an eyebrow, and Susan continued, 'He saved me, rescued me, hid me more than once and allowed me to heal. He's even forgiven me for wanting to take my own life. You have to love someone a lot to do that for them. So, the least I can do is help those who are in difficulty and show them the love that He showed me.'

They spent a week together working out how the system would work in order to protect the identity of those looking for safety. Elsa and Susan also showed him some of the sights around Huntersville over the weekend. When it was time for Mister Henderson to return to his office, she shook hands with him at the railway station and thanked him for all his hard work.

He hugged her in return and said: 'Since we are going to working together on this, you might as well call me Gary.'

That night, her last thought before she slept was, *Lord, you're the God that gives hope, and I pray for all those you're going to give hope to through my pain.*

What Susan wasn't to know at that moment was that Elsa would leave her the home that she had purchased and between them, Gary, Elsa, and herself, they would give many men and women, both young and old, a second chance at life.

Barry

It was one of those mornings when Barry couldn't help but be thankful for his life. It had rained the night before and the mist was rising off the river. The heat of summer was starting to give way to winter. He loved this time of year, probably more so than Spring. In spring, there was just so much work to be done, that there was little time to appreciate the new life that was happening around him, whereas in Autumn, things were starting to wind down. You had time to stop and bask in the satisfaction of a job, or many jobs, well done. Winter was a hard slog for him, particularly now as he was older, he found it hard to get up in the cold to milk the cows. Oh, how he wished that his son had lived, he'd have been able to relinquish the reins to him by now.

He gave himself a mental shake. There was no use wishing his life away. Sorry Lord, I shouldn't be doing that, but I don't understand your plan in all of this. My service for you seems so insufficient for all the good things that have outweighed our grief.

As he opened the gate to round up the cows for milking, he remembered coming out with his father most mornings to help him bring in the cows. He always looked forward to the father and son time they had. In the quiet of the morning, they had talked about all sorts of things, this was the best time to talk to his father about those big questions of life that bothered a growing young lad. If he remembered correctly, the first question, after someone had stolen his favourite dog, had been about why God let bad things happen. His father had explained that God gave everyone the choice to do the right or wrong thing. 'Would you like it if I tied you to the end of a rope and dragged you around the paddock to help me bring the cows in?'

'No.'

'So, why do you come with me?'

'I love you and want to be with you as much as I can, but it's nice to know that I can stay in bed if I'm sick.'

'Let me tell you, I'd rather have you come with me because you want to, rather than being grumpy because you have to. I think you learn more about farming that way and I guess God wants it that way too.'

'Then, there was the time he'd been to church with his mother and the preacher's sermon had been on how important it was to gather together with other Christians. On the way home, it had bothered him so much that his father didn't attend church most Sundays, that he had said something to his mother about how he was worried that his father wasn't saved and would go to hell if he died. She had smiled, told him that his father was the most dedicated Christian that she knew, and that he should talk to his father about it. So, the next morning, while they were getting the cows, he'd asked.

'Dad, why don't you go to church? The preacher said yesterday that we shouldn't forget to gather together in fellowship'

'Son, I have too many jobs to do. If I took time out to travel all that way into church, I wouldn't get the cows milked, or the pigs, chooks, and sheep fed, but I don't forget to have fellowship with God's saints. Your mother has to be the greatest saint I know, and when I go to town, I make sure that I engage in fellowship with all those that I meet. What I do know, is that it's more important for me to have fellowship with God himself, and I do that every day while I'm working out here in His very own cathedral.'

'So, why do you make me go?'

'Because you need to hear what others say, like the preacher, so you can test it out for yourself and develop your own relationship with God. If you hadn't been to church, would you have asked me why I didn't go? This is what fellowship is about. I spend a lot of time praising God every time I see the birth of a calf, piglet, or lamb. Each time it rains, I thank God for His blessings. Besides, by going to church, you get to meet people your own age, how else are you going to find someone to marry and share the blessings of God with?'

Looking back now, he realized that his father had been pretty smart. Most Monday mornings his father would ask him if there was anything from Sunday's sermon that he was concerned about, and in this way, he had made sure that he actually listened to the preacher so they could talk about the lessons while they were working together. He remembered the morning he had talked about women being the weaker vessel. His father had almost choked.

"Son, I really wish Peter had used a different word in that passage. As I see it, men are clay pots, but women are vessels made of fine china. Sure, your mother can't lift the bags of wheat or bales of hay, but let me tell you, there is no way on this green earth that I could go through the pain of childbirth. She is the one that helps me get up and carry on when I struggle to face another day, particularly in the winter. They should be treated with care, not because they are weaker, but because they are so much more precious and beautiful."

Barry had to agree with his father, once he had fallen in love with his wife. He learnt very quickly just how strong and courageous she was. They'd had a son, who was the greatest bundle of energy he'd ever laid eyes on. His wife was way more patient with him as a toddler than he ever was, and when it came to giving into his tantrums, her determination to stand firm made him feel feeble. When their son was in his early teens, he had suddenly fallen sick, sadly the doctors hadn't been able to work out what was wrong, and he had died.

They had managed to carry on with their new normal, and again he saw the strength that his wife was endowed with rise to the surface. She not only carried herself through that time but had also managed to help him slowly lift himself out of the pit of despair that surrounded him.

As the cows moved into the yard, ready to be milked, Barry gave himself another mental shake. What was wrong with him this morning? Anyone would think that he was about to meet his maker with all this reminiscing, but maybe it was part of the grief process, they had received a letter, just two days ago, to say that his wife's sister had lost her husband in a farming accident.

They had decided that she would take the night train to Huntersville, a town in the middle of nowhere, to visit her in a couple of days' time. He'd liked the bloke; he'd had a great sense of humour, making him easy to get along with.

At breakfast he was still thinking about his father when his wife, tapped him on the shoulder, he looked at her, 'Sorry, love. Did you say something?'

'Yes, are you alright?'

'Yeah, but for some reason I keep visiting my walks with dad this morning.'

'It's probably got something to do with Terry dying and facing your own mortality.'

'I can't believe it's taken this long for her to let us know about the accident.'

'Now, Barry. Be fair. She would have been very busy looking after Terry and trying to keep things going on the farm. When would she have had time to write? Plus, the time the mail takes to get around. Besides, she wouldn't have wanted us to worry. After all, she knows there is no-one here to look after this place and that you would have jumped in the car to try and help, but that's not practical, is it?'

'No, you're right.'

'Besides, I'm leaving the day after tomorrow to go and see her, just to make sure that she is okay. What I'm concerned about is how you're going to manage for two whole weeks without me.'

'I'll be fine, I won't starve, even if I end up living on bread and butter and eggs, anyway, I've got plenty stored up here.' He smiled at her while patting his ample middle.

'Yeah, I know you'll be fine, but that brings me back to my original question. What time do you want to leave to go to town? I've got a few things that I need to get before I leave and today would be the best day to get them.'

'That's a good idea, give me two hours, and enough time to change my clothes and we'll be off. I'll even treat you to lunch at that new café in town. It'll save you having to pack something for us, how's that?'

'Oh, that would be nice, have I told you lately that I love you?'

Barry looked thoughtful for a long time, finally he smiled, 'Umm, Oh yes, I think it was the first thing you said to me this morning, but please tell me again.'

She giggled and playfully swatted him on the shoulder. 'You'd better go and get those jobs done, or else we'll be too late to do anything, let alone have lunch.'

'You're right as usual, I'll see you in a couple of hours.' He kissed her and walked out the door feeling much brighter than he had when he had started his breakfast.

Later that day, while his wife was finishing some of her dealings with the storekeeper, he was sitting on a bench outside the shop, observing the people in the street. One couple, in particular, grabbed his attention. The gentleman was very tall and broad shouldered, the woman much shorter and petite. Well, that's certainly the tall and the short of it, he thought. Dad's description of clay pot and fine china certainly fits that couple. As he was watching, the woman stumbled, dropping the bag that she was carrying. Barry looked on with horror as the man snarled at her about being clumsy, grabbed her arm, dragged her towards a car parked nearby, and almost threw her into it. The woman briefly looked at him while the man raced around the other side, jumped in, and quickly drove off. What Barry noticed most was the despair in the woman's eyes. That look stayed with him for the rest of the day. He had prayed several times for her saying: 'Lord, I don't know who she is or who the man is, but please, I know you know who they are, and Lord, please keep her safe because I believe that she is in real danger, and if there is anything I can do, Lord, I am willing.'

Her face haunted him on and off during the next day, and he was quietly saying a prayer for her as he walked out with a heavy heart to bring the cows in for the evening milking. They weren't in their usual paddock, so he set about trying to find them. Eventually he discovered that they were down near the river.

'Goodness me, what are you lot doing down here? What on earth possessed you to stray into this paddock? Come on, girls, time to let me have some of that milk, it'll make you feel better, you know that.' He chatted away to the cows as he moved them along the bank. They hadn't gone very far when something caught his eye on the edge of the river. On investigation, it turned out to be a woman, not just any woman, but the one that he had seen the day before in town, being dragged into the car by the tall bloke.

'Oh, God, I think she's dead. I asked you to keep her safe. Why didn't you do that? Well, at least he can't hurt her anymore, so I guess you answered my prayer after all.' However, as he got closer, he realised that, surprisingly, she was still alive but boy, she was pretty banged up. He reached down and gently lifted her out of the river. As soon as she opened her eyes, she started begging him not to tell anyone that she was still alive. He carried her back to the house, all the while telling her that she was safe and that they would do what they could to keep her that way. 'Oh, Lord, this woman is your daughter and I know that you love her. Help us to show her the love that comes from you and Lord, I ask that you cover her with the wings of your angels,' he prayed.

The other remarkable thing that happened on that short journey, as he carried her home to his wife, was that the father in him became angry for her. She was someone's daughter, but it seemed that they hadn't taken care of her, why else would she be in this state? His father-heart broke for the pain she had experienced, and in doing so, it adopted her as the daughter they never had. Once inside, he allowed his wife to take over. He knew that her nursing experience from before their marriage would kick in. While he waited to see how she was, he stoked up the fire, made tea, and prayed, 'Father God, you are the healer of all that is broken, please mend this child of yours so that she

28

knows that you love her and have a plan for her life'. He found another cup, filled it with tea, stirring in two large spoonfuls of sugar, and handed it to her when they emerged from their son's vacant room.

He left the two women together while he returned to the milking. Later, while she slept, he and his wife discussed what needed to be done. His wife had discovered that her name was Susan and that the man who Barry had seen treating her so badly the day before was indeed her husband, and in order to protect her from further bad treatment, they decided that she should travel with his wife when she visited her sister. Hopefully, her sister, having lost her husband, would be willing to let Susan stay on at the farm to help her. The problem was how to hide her from those at the station who might recognise her. Barry casually dropped the comment that she looked no bigger than their son had been when he died. His wife had looked at him thoughtfully, and said, 'You know, I think if we dress her in some of Barry Junior's clothes and hide her hair, she might pass for a young lad, particularly with his big coat on. That might be the way to hide who she really is. They knew that her middle name was Joanne so it was decided that they would call her Jo, to complete the disguise.'

And so, the plan had been implemented.

He had seen them off at the station and spent the next two weeks praying hard, not only for his wife's sister and Susan, but that his wife would return home alone.

The day she was to return, he went to the station to collect her and was very relieved to find that she was the only one who alighted from the train.

As he hugged her in welcome, he whispered, 'The visit went well?'

'Yes, Jo worked hard and couldn't learn things fast enough. I think it will be good for Elsa to have Jo staying there.'

'Praise God.'

That night, as he lay in bed, he had his regular conversation with God. 'Lord, I'm sure you're going to do great things through Susan. Thank you for letting us be a small part of that.'

What Barry didn't know that night, was that in a few months, during a storm, there would be a car accident on the road right near his home. As his wife rode the horse to get help, he would try to assist the occupants. What would surprise him was that the driver would be the husband of Susan Landtry, the woman he'd taken to his heart as a daughter, and that he was already dead. The elderly couple in the back were still alive, and he would pray with them and be happy to hear them ask God for His forgiveness just before they took their last breaths. He would then sit down in the middle of the road as tears of grief, joy, and relief would flow, mingled with the rain that washed over him. His grief would be for a soul lost to hell for eternity, the joy, for the couple who found the love of God just before death grabbed their final chance, and the utter relief was that Susan was now finally, truly, safe.

Gary

Gary Henderson looked at the documents sitting on his desk. The details of the trust, set up with the Landtry family assets, was finalised. He sighed and smiled with satisfaction. He went over the discussions that he'd had with Susan Landtry over his week-long stay at Huntersville. He had sat and listened to her story of how she had tried to drown herself in the river after Michael had taken his fury out on her the night before and early that morning. She also told him the reasons why she wanted to use the proceeds from the family's estate to set up this trust. They had discussed many of the problems that they knew existed, after all, if it wasn't for the farmer and his wife dressing her in their son's clothes, he himself would have recognised her when he got on the same train as she did two days after the fire. He told her how he had almost said hello, except that Constable Davis had told him that, even if there was no body, Susan would be considered deceased. He too, it seems, had felt powerless to do anything to save her and he determined that this way she would be safe. They deliberated about solutions to the problems they could foresee and trusted God to help them with the ones that they couldn't. If he was honest with himself, he'd admit that he was really enjoying the cloak and dagger nature that this work would require. Is this how those that rescued slaves in America felt? He had never married, so this gave him some extra excitement that wasn't found in his regular work. It was a good cover really, his regular job required that he present himself as a boring, dull, and upright citizen.

What he hadn't told Susan, was that there was another very good reason for him to help her in her quest.

His own father had died when he was only eight years old. His mother had taken work as a cleaner to get enough money to make sure that there was food on the table and that he and his bother got a very good education. When his older brother had turned sixteen he assumed the responsibility of man of the house, which had puzzled Gary, as things seemed to be going along reasonably smoothly except that his mother was always tired, but given that the number of hours she worked, it was expected. It wasn't until he returned home after being away at school that he noticed things weren't what they should be. To start with, he noticed that his mother seemed unhappy, and what seemed strange was that, even in the summer heat, she always wore a long-sleeved top.

One day he had come into the kitchen, where she was doing the dishes, without her noticing. Her sleeves were rolled up and he caught a glimpse of a number of bruises, his involuntary gasp made her jump, as she quickly pulled her sleeves down. When he had asked her how she got them she insisted that she had bumped into the doorframe during the night while she was getting some water. Something about what she said didn't sit right with him, but she had doggedly stuck to her story. He kept a much closer eye on her after that and noticed that his older brother seemed to be putting pressure on his mother to give him whatever took his fancy. While he didn't witness any actual volent acts while they were together, he noticed that his mother was very careful around his brother.

Two days before his mother died, he just happened to be walking past one of the windows and caught his brother pushing his mother, she fell hard. Gary had taken her to the hospital and discovered that there were a lot more bruises all over her body, so he sat by her bedside for the two days talking to her and comforting her as best as he could. The doctors had ruled her death as an accidental fall and when he had suggested that his brother was responsible, they had ignored him, and accepted his brother's convincing explanation.

When they had visited the solicitor after the funeral, he was to discover that the house and all her possessions had been willed to his brother, as the eldest. He had accepted the terms of the will but had walked out of that office vowing to become a solicitor and to make sure that he would try and protect as many people as he could. However, he had discovered that it was more difficult to execute that vow than to make it. Now, thanks to Susan, he could finally start to make good on that promise.

There was one other duty that Susan had asked him to carry out as soon as any money was available and that was to present Barry, the farmer who had pulled her out of the river, with enough money to buy the new tractor they desperately needed. The look of gratitude on the faces of husband and wife, when he'd been to see them, was one very good memory he intended to hang on to.

Barry had told him how he had witnessed Michael's treatment of Susan in the street and how the next day the cows has wandered off down to the river, and that he believed that God allowed them to go there so that he would find Susan. He also told him about the accident a couple of months earlier and that he had prayed with Michael's parents, having found Michael already dead when he arrived. They had written to Elsa to tell them all this, but the postal service, as reliable as it was, was extremely slow that far out.

Maybe, now that the trust had been set up, he would be able to get rid of the memory that had haunted him for all those months after Susan Landtry had supposedly died in the fire that burnt down her home. That sad look in her eyes the night before when he had been talking to her at the party.

If he was honest with himself, he knew, in fact all their friends knew, that Michael wasn't treating Susan with the tenderness that she was entitled to. Society, however, dictated that a man owned his wife and that he was entitled to treat her in whatever manner he considered necessary, and no-one came between a man and his wife, it just wasn't done.

Even on the day of the fire, he hadn't bought the story that Susan had perished, not really, there was nothing left of the building except some rickety, smouldering timbers. The day after the fire, he'd been talking with the investigating officer, Constable Davis, who was also an acquaintance of the family, and he had told him quietly that, even if he didn't find a body, officially she was deceased.

'How are you going to pull that off?'

'Well, burnt bodies are not recognisable and it's unthinkable to put people as sensitive as the Landtry's through such a grotesque procedure as identifying the body, besides, the right number of rocks make a good substitute for a body in a closed coffin.'

'You would do that? If you're found out, they'll kill you.'

'I doubt if they will ever find out; Susan's not going to come back here, is she? No woman should be treated the way she was, but there was nothing even I could do, the law was on his side.'

'So true. Do you have any idea where she might be?'

'No idea. We've checked with her parents and what few friends she did have, and they haven't seen her. We even went through their houses to make sure they weren't hiding her, that's what the law requires of us.' He paused before he continued. 'You know what! I don't want to know. To be honest with you, I hope she managed to get out of the country, but I'm pretty sure that the family have friends watching all the ports. She was like a bird trapped in a cage, which was beaten regularly.'

The next day, he'd been on the train travelling to the city to see a client, when he noticed a woman and a young man get on. There was something very odd about the young man though. He didn't walk like a man and could have been easily mistaken for a young lady.

"Here, Joe, these are our seats." The woman said, and another gentleman, kissed her on the cheek, shook the young person's hand and said, "May the Lord go with you," as he left the train. At the time he had wondered if that person was really Susan in disguise and part of him wanted to know, but the words of Constable Davis rang in his ears. It was better for her if he didn't know. Goodness knows how long her husband would live, and if she was forced to return home, things would be even worse for her a second time around, of that he was sure. He'd relaxed in his seat and tried to get some sleep, but Susan's sad face at that party continued to haunt his dreams. He had left the train in the middle of the night, so he had no idea at which station they got off.

He had become firm friends with the Constable after that encounter, and they watched the Landtry family quietly, and with interest, from the sidelines. They noticed that Michael's alcohol consumption increased, his parent's too, they didn't seem to even try and hide their bad behaviour and most people started to distance themselves from the family. He had declined to take any phone calls from them, citing a full workload, trying to delay any work to their wills for as long as possible. If anything happened as a result of their self-destructive behaviour, Susan would still inherit any residual monies, that is, assuming that she could be found. It didn't take too much imagination to realise that these people were unlikely to live to an old age.

The morning Mister Henderson received the call from Constable Davis to inform him that all members of the family had died in a car accident the night before, was one that he would never forget. He must have sat in his chair for nearly an hour, feeling relieved that these people could no longer inflict pain on anyone else.

After placing two notices in several newspapers, one: the death notice for the family, and the other asking Jo Landtry to contact him, he wasn't totally surprised to receive hundreds of letters from people indicating that they were Jo Landtry. When he opened Susan's letter, he knew that he had finally found the person he was really looking for. On the notepaper was an address in a town he'd never heard of before and the Bible reference, Luke 4:10.

He didn't know his Bible all that well, but when he looked it up, he was very sure that this person was in fact Susan Landtry. It read: "For it is written, He shall give his angels charge over thee, to keep thee:" that was the verse that she had referred to at the party they had attended the night before she had disappeared.

He checked his watch, nearly closing time. *Good*, he thought as he gathered up the necessary paperwork and made his way to the reception desk. He told his secretary that he needed to go away for an extended business trip, and gave her the task of, not only cancelling all his appointments until he returned, but also replying to all the false letters regarding the existence of Jo Landtry while he was away. He walked out of the building, purchased his ticket to Huntersville, packed his bag and was ready to board the train when it pulled into the station, three hours later.

As he emerged from Huntersville station, he noticed that the bakery was nearly directly opposite, next to a rather grand looking pub. He booked in under the name of David Brown and then walked next door. As he entered, the older lady who turned around to serve him had a familiar look about her. She certainly wasn't the woman from the train but could easily have been a relative. He'd always had a good memory for faces.

He explained his reason for being there and she showed him into the kitchen attached to the shop. He'd been pleased to find that Susan was looking so well, and she wanted to use her inheritance to help people who found themselves in similar circumstances. It was amazing to see that she hadn't become bitter, instead, here she was really wanting to help others and it was kind of fitting that the estate of the family who had caused so much grief was going to be put to such good.

He had determined that, from now on, he would have the courage to step in and make sure that others in her circumstances were taken care of. There were a lot of details that needed to be worked through and he indicated that, once he had figured out some of the finer details, he would be back to check if she was happy about the arrangements. One thing they did establish was that urgent communications would need to be made by telegram using an agreed code, rather than phone calls, simply because staff on the phone exchange had ears and could not always be trusted to be deaf, let alone silent. All other communication needed to be by confidential letter. He couldn't even risk making too many visits to this town just in case someone got suspicious.

On his return home, he had spoken to Constable Davis, and between them, they had hatched a plan. Gary told him about seeing Susan on the train two days after the fire and they realised that sending victims on the train as passengers would not always be a good idea. Constable Davis had enlisted the help of some friends and they had a box made up that could be used to hide people in, thereby enabling them to travel in the baggage car. It was risky, but the guard at the station had also been on the receiving end of bad behaviour and was prepared to help others. Gary had written to Susan giving her details of the plan and she had written by return correspondence that the guard at their station was also a kind man and was prepared to make sure that the box was unloaded carefully.

He looked back down at the papers still sitting on his desk. Well, now they could start to help some people and he wondered for a minute who would be the first person to secure their freedom. First though, he needed to tell Susan that things had been finalised and that from now on, if it was at all possible, they would be able to help those in need. He sent her a telegram, as prearranged, it said one word. "Ready".

That night, he prayed, 'Lord, you're a wonderful God. Thank you for giving us the means of helping those who suffer the same pain that Susan did'. He slept very well that night, and for the first time in a year, wasn't haunted by the look on Susan's face at the party.

What he didn't know, was that in a few weeks he would assist Barbara Simpson to escape from her son and daughter-in-law, and after years of writing to her and a few visits, he would enjoy his retirement in Huntersville, married to Barbara, where he would take up oil painting.

Barbara

Barbara entered Mister Henderson's office. She could feel Eric's hand tighten on her arm. She was tired, very tired. Since Eric had married Grace, he had become increasingly hard to live with. Grace, having sacked the household staff to save money, had decided that it was Barbara's job to look after the house and the business while ever the business was legally under her control. Both Eric and Grace spent much of their time sleeping and attending parties at night. Her husband had been worried that Eric hadn't had enough time to learn the business and that he wasn't mature enough to take the lead. She knew that he would be horrified about the way she was being treated but she just didn't have the strength to fight anymore.

Mister Henderson stood up as they entered his office. 'Thank you, Sadie', he said to his secretary and turned to Barbara. "It's nice to see you Missus Simpson. Are you well? I hadn't heard that you were ill.' She knew that she had lost weight, Grace was very strident about the amount of food that she could eat. Once upon a time she had taken a lot of pride in her appearance, but right now, she just didn't have the energy to do more than make sure that her clothes were clean, she didn't even have the get-up-and-go to make sure that they fitted neatly. She was aware, that if someone passed her on the street, they might mistake her for a vagrant. 'Eric, Grace,' Mister Henderson voice cut into her thoughts as he nodded to the other two, 'please take a seat.'

He sat in his own chair and looked at them but seemed to be thinking about something else for a few minutes. He brought his attention back to them, making Barbara feeling a little uncomfortable. How was she going to be able to get through this meeting without making Eric and Grace angrier than they already were? These two were very careful to make sure that there were no bruises that could be seen to indicate that they were treating her badly. Her punishment was mostly dished out by means of removing her food from the table or her blankets off her bed. It was the taunts about her being old, silly, and selfish that hurt her the most. She noticed that Mister Henderson was watching her carefully.

'My mother would like to make changes to her will.' Eric said. Mister Henderson looked straight at her, and she looked away.

He turned to Eric, 'Well, it's usual for me to speak to the client alone, so how about you retire to the waiting room, I'll get my secretary to provide you with some refreshments while we discuss our business.' Neither of the children made a move. Fixing his gaze on them, he waited. 'Do I need to ask Constable Davis to assist you? Because I will have you charged with trespass if you don't do as I ask.' His voice left no room for argument.

The couple looked at each other, and slowly walked out of the room. Sadie closed the door firmly behind them, and Barbara felt herself relax just a little bit.

'Well, Missus Simpson, what can I do for you?'

'Mister Henderson, Eric has become very insistent that its time I let him run the business. Gary reached across the table to pat her hand as an act of compassion and noticed her flinch, almost involuntarily. Suddenly, it was as if he was looking at his mother again.

'What do you want?' he asked with a voice full of compassion.

'Mister Henderson, I am tired. He can have the business, but I wish I didn't have to stay, as they will probably insist that I keep doing all the housework and they just don't seem to be able to put anything away. They leave a mess wherever they go. I know it's not what my husband wanted but I feel powerless to stop it. Last night, I was reading about how Phillip was spirited away after he was speaking to the Ethiopian, and I found myself wishing that I could be taken away just like that.' She smiled weakly at Gary.

He leaned forward and rested his arms on the desk. 'Are they hitting you?'

'No, I sometimes wish they were, at least I would have some evidence of what they are like. Please, Mister Henderson, is there any way out of this mess?'

Gary sat back in his chair thoughtfully, 'What would you take with you if you were able to leave?'

'All I want to take is a small photo of my husband, everything else they can have.'

'Do you have the photo with you?' Barbara nodded, 'I carry it with me all the time, in case they decide that it's rubbish.'

'Alright, I'll draw up the papers for Eric to sign. When he comes back in here, I will tell them that they need to go home for a couple of hours while my secretary types up the necessary papers. I want you to go with them, so they don't think anything unusual is happening. I suggest that you put a couple of layers of clothes on under your coat and in the meantime, I will arrange for you to disappear into thin air.'

'You can do that?' For the first time since she had walked into his office, she felt hope rising up inside her. 'How?'

'Missus Simpson, at this point, the less you know, the safer you will be. Oh, one other thing, are you afraid of small spaces?' She shook her head.

'Good.' He picked up the phone, when it was answered he said, 'It's time for the trust box to be collected', and hung up.

Gary looked at Missus Simpson, 'Well, let's bring the kids back in,' he pressed the button on the intercom and asked Sadie to collect Eric and Grace.

Once they returned, he indicated that they sit down. 'Okay, I have been given my instructions from your mother, however, it will take a couple of hours for the paperwork to be prepared.' Barbara felt Eric silently cheering.

'It can be done that quickly?'

41

'Yes, but let me finish, please. As I said, it will take a couple of hours to prepare the paperwork. I strongly suggest that you return home. Your mother looks as if she could use a good rest. When you return, she will sign the paperwork and I will go over it and through the conditions with you. Then once you have signed the papers, the company will be under your control.'

They stood up, 'Okay, sure, we will see you in a couple of hours then.' It was evident that Eric couldn't get out of the office fast enough. He grabbed his mother's arm. 'Come on mum, the sooner we get out of here, the sooner Mister Henderson can see to the paperwork'.

A couple of hours later, the family returned to the office. Sadie again showed Eric and Grace into a vacant office. Constable Davis was entering an office further along the hallway and said hello to Sadie. Mister Henderson had met Barbara himself and directed her into his office. He sat in his chair, 'Are you sure this is what you want?'

'Of course it isn't, but I just can't see any other way out of this situation. I honestly feel as if I'm being unfaithful to my husband, but there are times when I just want to die. I'm not an old person really and I feel as if there has to be more to life than cleaning up after my selfish child, and yes, I find that very hard to admit, Mister Henderson, I have failed as a mother and also as a wife, however, I have to admit, that Eric wasn't like this before he married Grace. Mister Henderson pushed the papers across the table, and she signed them. When she had finished, she looked up at him sadly. 'I'm glad my husband isn't alive to see this.'

'Ma'am, if he had been alive, it wouldn't have come to this, of that I'm sure, but now leave things to me. I know where I can find you and I will come and visit you when I can. Okay, are you ready?'

'Yes, what happens now?'

'Constable Davis will deliver you to the railway station, where you will be placed in a comfortable box, and loaded on to the train. We can't risk you being recognised by anyone during the journey. There are air-holes so you will have plenty of ventilation. It will be delivered to a young lady who understands your position. You can stay there for as long as you need. I'm due to visit her in a few weeks, so I'll be able to see how you are doing then. As far as the kids are concerned, you are having refreshments until we get to the part of the document that says that they are not to try and find you or they will forfeit control of the business to me. That should work.'

She stood up; Mister Henderson did the same thing. As she passed by, in a moment of foolishness, she turned and hugged him, blushing, she said, 'Thank you so much.'

'You are most welcome, now please go with Constable Davis. You can't afford to miss that train.'

At the station, the Constable spirited her into the guard's office and assisted her into a large wooden box. The lid was closed It was nearly dark anyway, so once the box was settled on the train, she closed her eyes and slept.

About mid-morning the next day, she was woken by someone knocking on the lid of the box. 'Are you okay?'

'Yes.'

'That's good, I'll let you out now.' As Barbara emerged from the box, she was greeted by the station guard and a young woman who seriously looked no older than a teenager, she smiled and said, 'Now that the train has moved on, we can leave for my house'.

Once they had arrived, Susan showed her the room in which Barbara would be staying. Barbara looked around and turned to Susan, who was standing in the doorway. 'Do you mind if I remove some of these extra clothes that I'm wearing. Mister Henderson suggested that I put on several layers.'

'That's fine, the kitchen is just through that door there, she pointed down the hallway. I'll get your meal ready.'

As Barbara entered the kitchen a few minutes later, she saw the surprised look on Susan's face.

'My goodness, we are going to have to feed you up and put some meat on those bones, how long since you had a decent meal?'

'Oh, about three years. The kids made sure that I got just enough to keep me from dying.'

'Well, we'll get you back on track soon enough. Now, please sit down and let us eat.'

'So, what do I need to do to repay you for your kindness?'

'Nothing.'

'What do you mean, nothing?'

'The whole point of bringing you here is to allow you time to rest and, in your case, get you up to a decent weight. The trust that Mister Henderson and I have set up is for exactly that purpose. Once you feel better, you can decide how you want to move on, but there is definitely no rush. One day, I'll tell you my story, but not right now, you look as if you should go and lay down.'

'Okay, it seems ridiculous, I've had the best sleep in such a long time and yet, I still feel tired.'

'It's fine, sleep is one of the ways God uses to help our bodies recover from trauma. Now, go, I'll come and wake you in time for tea.'

For the first week, Barbara did little else other than sleep and eat.

After that, she helped Susan around the house, doing only light duties. During that time, she heard Susan's story and met Elsa, the woman who Susan credited with saving her life.

She had been there for six weeks when there was a knock at the front door; Susan answered and brought Mister Henderson into the kitchen. He smiled at Barbara, 'Well, you certainly look in much better health than the last time we met. I hope you are feeling much better.'

'I am, thanks to Susan's good cooking and lots of sleep. How did things go with Eric and Grace after I left?'

'Let's have a cup of tea', Susan injected, 'the man has had a long journey'.

'Oh, I'm sorry, how thoughtless of me.'

'It's okay, it is one of the reasons that I have come all this way, apart from bringing Susan up-to-date on some details of the trust.'

Over that cuppa, and like always, these things turned out to be a meal, rather than just a cup of tea, Mister Henderson told them how, when Eric and Grace had returned to the office, he had told them that she was out getting some refreshments. 'I didn't lie, they just weren't the refreshments that they thought I was referring to. I went through the agreement with them, and then I got to the final clause, which told them that they would need to present a financial statement to me every month, for me to audit, for which I would be charging them a small fee and if I found that the business wasn't being run properly then I would be taking over and they wouldn't have any choice but to do exactly what I dictate. Eric looked very angry and asked, where you were and I told them that you were away getting some long-term refreshments, so they had got exactly what they wanted. You would no longer be involved in the business, or available to carry out the housework, so they would need to start to do all the work themselves, and if they ever tried to find you, they would be put in jail for fraud. Eric almost jumped across the table threatening to call the police. At that point, I pressed the intercom and said, "Let me help you out there." I asked my secretary to let Constable Davis in. He knocked on the door and entered. "Is everything okay, would you like me to charge this man with assault?" I looked at Eric and asked, "Well, are you going to sign this paper quietly and get on with life without your mother, or do I have you charged with assault?" Eric had sat down and signed without any more fuss. Constable Davis had one of his men watch the house for a couple of days and he reported that they had a big fire in the backyard, we can only assume that they burnt all the clothes that belonged to you.'

Mister Henderson then handed Barbara an envelope, 'I have completed their first audit; so far, they seem to be doing the right thing. Here is your share of the audit fee. I've kept one pound, as my collection fee, and to cover the time it took to look at the books. I will be sending you future payments in the mail, as much as I would like to visit each month and hand you the money in person, I still want to be careful, for the moment, just in case they decide to follow me. I'm pretty sure that they were watching me for the week after that audit, hoping that I would lead them to you. I wouldn't put it past them to arrange an accident for you.'

That night, while the ladies were enjoying a drink on the verandah in the cool of the evening, Barbara looked at Susan, 'What do I do now?' The money Mister Henderson gave me will only go so far. I really do need to do something with the rest of my life.'

'What do you enjoy doing most?'

'Actually, sewing, but this is such a small town, I'm thinking there's not much call for a seamstress around here.'

'This town supplies a much larger area than just the few houses that you see. There are a lot of farmers that come to town for their supplies. I think it might be a good idea to go and see Mister Green who owns the Mercantile. He might be able to send work your way. There's a small living quarters behind the bakery, which we own, where you could stay. Elsa can move back into the house here for a little while.'

'But that would mean that you won't have room for the next person that needs to use the bedroom.'

'Let's not worry about that for the moment. Go and see Mister Green first and see what he has to say. He's the only one who knows what sort of market there is for your skills.'

Two days later, Barbara was in the Mercantile shopping for some new ribbon to update one of the dresses that she had managed to bring with her. Now that she had a small amount of money, she finally felt the freedom to actually do something that she liked. At the counter, she asked the girl behind it who she would go to if she wanted a new dress made. The girl looked at her, 'Well, the only person who was doing it for other people told Mister Green just yesterday that they wouldn't be taking on any more work, her arthritis is getting too painful for her to sew anymore.'

'Is Mister Green available for me to speak to?'

'Yes, I'll just get him, can I tell him who is asking for him?'

'Barbara.'

'Barbara who?'

'Just Barbara. Tell him I'm a friend of Susan Landtry, please.'

'Oh, alright.'

She returned a few minutes later followed by a much older man.

'I'm just wondering if you might be able to let people know that I am a seamstress and I'm looking for work.'

'Sure thing, but how do I know if you do a good job?'

'I'll bring something in tomorrow that I've made if that would suit.'

'Yeah, sure.' But Barbara could see that he didn't seem too impressed.

As promised, Barbara returned to the store not long after he had opened the doors for business; she handed him the dress that she had been wearing the day before.

'Why didn't you tell me you made this?'

'I wanted you to inspect the workmanship, something you wouldn't have been able to do while I was wearing it, however, you now know that what I make is made to fit.'

'Yes, this work looks very impressive. Well, Barbara, I think we can get you enough work, but it will take some time for people to get to know you, you haven't been in town for very long, are you planning on staying?'

'I have nowhere else to go, not for the foreseeable future. I have one problem to solve, however, I wasn't able to bring my sewing machine with me. The lady who isn't able to do sewing anymore, do you think I might be able to borrow her machine just until I save enough money to buy my own?'

'I have to make a delivery to her home this afternoon, so I will ask.'

'Thank you.'

She returned to Susan's home and told her what had taken place. Later, while they were enjoying afternoon tea, there was a knock on the back door. When Susan opened it, there stood Mister Green. 'I have a sewing machine for Barbara.'

Susan offered him a cup of tea once he had installed the machine in the front room of the house. 'This will do until Elsa moves back in here and Barbara moves into the living quarters of the bakery. She needs to have the freedom to work, sleep, and eat on her own timetable, not mine.'

'Oh, I wish there was somewhere else for me to live. I feel so bad for Elsa. She's such a kind lady. It's a pity that this house isn't bigger. I'm going to pray that God will give us a better answer than me pushing her out of her home.'

Barbara noticed that Mister Green had a thoughtful look on his face as he remarked. 'Well, the Bible says that God has the answer before we ask.'

'I hope you are right, Mister Green.'

The next day, Elsa arrived to see Susan. 'It seems that I won't have to move back in here with you after all' she said.

'Why ever not?' Susan asked surprised.

'Mister Green came to see me last night and asked me to marry him.'

'What?'

'Yes, we have had some interesting conversations over cups of tea while I've been staying behind the bakery. As you know, he has his own living quarters upstairs above the store. So, once we get married, I'll move into his home. That way Barbara can move in behind the bakery, and you will still have the room here available for anyone that needs it.'

'Does that mean you won't be able to help out in the shop anymore?'

'I informed Mister Green that I wouldn't be giving up work. Afterall, he knows that I'm used to working hard on the farm and now the shop, even with this bad leg of mine. He's happy for me to keep helping out. I told him that we couldn't expect you to work from four am to six at night on your own, and he agreed.'

'Well, he was right about God having the answer. When are you going to get married?'

'We're seeing Reverend Smith after church on Sunday. We won't be waiting very long. We're too old to have a regular year-long engagement.' Elsa paused, looked at Barbara and continued. 'Barbara, would you make my dress for me, please. I'm sorry but I don't think you are going to have more than a few weeks to make it though. I don't want anything fancy but Harold insists that I get a new one.'

'No problem. Simple dresses can look stunning.'

As it turned out, Barbara moved into the bakery the next day, Elsa stayed with Susan until the wedding, allowing Barbara to make Elsa's dress. The night after the wedding, Barbara lay in bed feeling a little bit lonely as she was thinking over the events that led up to them all reaching this special day. God, you're so amazing. The way you move people and circumstances so that the answers to our problems are ready and waiting for us before they exist is truly astounding.

What Barbara couldn't see right then, was that God was already preparing for her future. She would successfully run the tailoring business and Mister Henderson would move to Huntersville, after his early retirement, and then she would again find companionship as his wife.

Eric

How did my life come to this? Eric lay on the hospital bed looking at the ceiling. His arm was itching where the drip was feeding the fluid into it, hopefully, in the end, giving him a second chance at life. During his time in hospital, he had watched other families interact with each other and their ill family members. What had struck him most, was how many of them were kind and caring, showing real concern about, not only the condition of those who were ill, but those who were having to watch their loved ones suffer. It had made him realise that Grace's treatment of him had been very much the opposite and their treatment of his mother had been appalling. Over the last few days, he had been remembering all the good things that had been part of his childhood and how much love his parents had showered on him, their only child.

Grace hadn't been to see him in the two weeks that he had been here. It now occurred to him that she might not really care for him in the way that she had told him she did over the years.

His memory rolled back to when he had first met her. He had been spending a bit of time with his father, who had insisted that Eric wear a suit and tie, at work. After the morning meetings, which he had sat in on, his father had sent him to the corner store to collect their lunch orders. Grace had been standing at the counter, apparently waiting for her order. She wasn't that pretty to look at, but then he always considered himself to be an average Joe in the looks department anyway. She had turned and watched him walk in, she had looked him up and down with real appreciation in her eyes and smiled as he stood beside her and that got his attention.

'So, the office boy has been sent out to get lunch?' she said with a smile.

'No, actually, the boss's son. This lunch is considered too important for just anyone to collect.' He returned.

'How so?'

'Big meeting with investors and it's going to send the business in a new direction.'

'Oh.'

The attendant behind the counter handed his order over, 'Here, Eric, this is yours. I've put it on your company's account.'

'Thanks,' he said as he lifted the large box of food from the counter, he turned to Grace and said 'bye,' and walked out.

He was hoping to see her again and determined in his head to come to work more often just in order to make it happen.

However, life often knocks you down, just as you think things are looking up and, in his case, the death of his father as a result of an accident during the next week, did just that. It was months before he was able to even go back to the shop, and to be honest, he hadn't given Grace another thought. Between the funeral and helping his mother take over the reins of the business, there was very little spare time. His mother had decided that, in the interests of saving both time and money, she'd pack their lunches before they left for work each morning, giving Eric no reason at all to return to the store.

Eventually, his mother started to feel comfortable with the day to day running of the business, and probably without realising what she was doing, pushed Eric away. Having found himself with more free time on his hands, he went to the shop one day to get a cuppa, and as he sat looking into thin air, Grace came in. She spotted him and came over. That was the beginning of their courtship, she was charming, following him everywhere, making comments that soothed his bruised ego, which he appreciated at the time because he felt that his mother didn't need him anymore.

Grace was in a hurry to get married but his mother refused to give her permission and so they dated for two years before they wed. Looking back now, he could see that things changed slowly after they got married. Grace would make comments about how his mother was doing things wrong or give looks that indicated that what his mother was doing wasn't approved of, her arguments had been very convincing as to why such things weren't correct in her eyes. Over the years this included his behaviour as well. It had started off with tears when things didn't go her way, to stamping her feet, slowly progressing to physical beatings with her fists.

Somewhere along the way, he started to take his frustrations and anger out on his mother. As he looked back, he realised that he wasn't game enough to stand up to Grace, so his mother was the one to suffer.

The fact that Grace hadn't been to see him in the last couple of weeks, made him realise that she was only interested in his money. She had got harder to live with once his mother had disappeared. He knew that the solicitor had done the right thing by removing his mother from the situation, but that had left him to deal with the abuse all by himself.

As he thought about things, it seemed to be poetic justice that he was now being treated for cancer. Thankfully, Grace wouldn't benefit from his death; Gary Henderson had made sure of that. On paper, with his demise, the business must be sold, and the proceeds would be held in trust for any direct living relatives. As they didn't have any children, it would mean that, if his mother was still alive, the funds would go to her, not Grace. He had suspected that Mister Henderson knew where his mother was all along.

The nurse came in to check his vital signs.

'Is there anything I can get you?' Her tone telling him that she felt a bit sorry for him.

'Can you ring Mister Henderson, the Solicitor, and ask if he would be willing to come and visit me, please?'

'Sure, I can do that.'

'Thanks.' He lay back and slept.

A couple of hours later the nurse came back in and told him that Mister Henderson would be in to see him the next day. He smiled at the nurse but didn't respond.

****

Mister Henderson entered the room the next morning. The movement woke Eric. He looked at the man that had saved his mother and wondered at the look of sympathy in his eyes.

'You know where mum is, don't you?'

'Yes, but I'm still not going to tell you, just in case Grace finds out.'

'That's alright, I don't want to know now. If I manage to beat this, then I'll worry about making restitution, but if I don't, would you please tell her that I'm really sorry for the way I treated her. Please, tell her that I have remembered the good things that she did for me when I was a child.'

'I could get my secretary, Sadie, to come in tomorrow and you can dictate a letter for your mother. I'm sure that she would much rather hear the words from you directly. If you wish, I will hold it until we know which way this situation plays out. But, if you'd rather not, I can certainly do that; your mother is a very special lady.' They continued to talk about some of the business issues.

Eric noticed how the solicitor's eyes lit up when his mother was mentioned. Suddenly, he realised that this man was in love with his mother. 'You will make mum happy one day,' he said, 'thank you for coming, I need to sleep now, but yes, could I dictate a letter to mum tomorrow?'

'Of course,' Mister Henderson stood up, he placed his hand on Eric's shoulder, 'I'll pray that you will get better soon, son', and walked out.

The next day the nurse came in to check his vitals and announce that there was a lady to see him. For one split second, he wondered if Grace had finally decided to visit him, then he saw Sadie standing in the doorway with a pen and notepad in her hands. Strangely, he didn't feel disappointment, but rather relief.

'Come on in.' he said, his voice much weaker than he expected it to sound.

Mister Henderson said that you wanted to dictate a letter to your mother, so, he's sent me to take it down. When I've typed it up, then he will bring it back for you to sign. It will be put away in the safe in accordance with your instructions.'

'Typed seems a bit impersonal, but I just don't have the strength to write it by hand.'

'Well, I'm not sure that she will understand my shorthand, but if you like, I will handwrite the letter out when I get back to the office, would that suit you better?'

Eric smiled, these people were so caring, even in their official capacity. What had he done to deserve this sort of treatment? Somewhere, deep in the recesses of his memories, he remembered a story about how a father had welcomed a long-lost son home after he had treated his family badly. Mister Henderson wasn't his father, but he was treating him with the same care that his own father would have.

'Eric?'

Sadie's voice brought him back to the present, he turned and looked at her.

'What would you like to say to your mother?'

'Oh,..... Dear mum. I want to say how sorry I am for the way we treated you. I have been doing some soul searching lately and I could blame it all on Grace, but in truth, I should have had the courage to stop her in the early days of our marriage. This letter is being dictated while I'm having treatment for cancer as I'm too weak to even write this myself.

I don't know if the treatment will work, so when you receive this letter, I will either have died, or recovered but moved away from Mount Grandsville, because living with Grace is no longer an option for me. I know that you have been living in seclusion all this time, and I am happy that you were able to get away from us. There is a temptation to come and live with you, but I feel that it is safer for us to not live in the same town. If things work out well, I may be able to come and visit for a short time if you are willing to see me again. I have talked to Mister Henderson in the last couple of days and told him of my wishes. I have also given him my blessing, not that he needs it, to pursue you sometime in the future. If this treatment doesn't work, I would have died knowing that you could be happy again with a man that cares so much for you. I can tell that he's interested in you as a person who shows strength and courage, which I now realise that you have in spades.

Again, I ask you to forgive me for the way we treated you. I have made my peace with God, and with this letter, I hope to have made my peace with you. Regardless of what happens to me, Mum, please be happy and live life to the fullest. That's what dad would have wanted for you and it's what I wish for you, despite what I did. Love Eric.

Do you think that's enough?'

'It sounds good to me, but I'll write it out nicely and then you can sign it, 'love Eric', yourself.'

'She's not to get this letter until I've died or moved away. If she knew I was sick she would be rushing back here to be with me, and I can't have her doing that. It wouldn't be fair, and she might run into Grace by accident and that shouldn't happen either. I need to have the courage that she has and get through this by myself.'

'Okay, if that's what you want.' Sadie closed her notebook. 'I'll get Mister Henderson to bring this back for you to sign tomorrow. Rest now.'

Sadie stood, and gently kissed his forehead, just like his mother would have, bringing tears to Eric eyes.

The next day, Mister Henderson returned with the letter neatly handwritten in Sadie's hand. He assisted Eric to sit up enough to sign his name. He wrote, carefully, *love Eric*, which Sadie had left off the bottom of the letter. Again, Mister Henderson spent time with him, and they talked about how his treatment was going. Eric also repeated his wishes about when his mother was to receive the letter and instructed him to continue to make sure that his mother received the audit money so that she wasn't alerted to something being wrong.

'How did you work out that your mother was getting some of that money?' Gary asked him.

'You're that sort of a man. Kind, honest, and I figured that she had to be living on something other than charity.'

'Well, it's nice to see that you've grown up quite a bit during this process, I have a feeling that your father would be proud of the man you have become, even with the detour along the way. I'll come back to visit you again in a couple of days, just to see how you are getting on.' Again, as he stood to leave, he placed his hand on Eric's shoulder and pressed it.

Eric closed his eyes and thought, if that man marries my mother, then, God, you're a God of justice.

In that moment, he still didn't know which of the two possible outcomes would be his reality. The drugs might work, and he would walk out of the hospital, and in a fantasy moment, he wondered if Sadie might have a place in that future. The other possibility was that the treatment didn't work, and he would die, but either way, knowing that he had made his peace with God, that his mother was safe, and that she would be happy with Mister Henderson, he decided that right now he could rest in peace.

Jessica

Jessica stood on the side of the road where her boyfriend had unceremoniously dumped her. They had been fighting a lot lately. Everything seemed to be getting out of control. He would walk away for a few hours and then return, telling her that he really loved her and somehow convince her that it had been all her fault, that she didn't understand him. Then somehow, she would give in, and he would have his way with her emotionally and physically. Now, it looked like she was carrying his child and today, she had, again, told him that she wasn't going to get rid of their baby. He had lost his temper, pulled over, opened the door, and told her to get out. She had watched him drive off down the road and around the bend. Surely, he would be back in five minutes; he really wouldn't actually leave her out here in the middle of nowhere all by herself, besides he always came back. Five minutes passed then ten and the sun was starting the burn her skin.

Maybe he was waiting for her to catch up. He will most likely be parked just around the bend out of sight. She started to walk, her shoes not really suitable for hiking but what choice did she have. Covering the distance as fast as she could, she was surprised to find that there was no car waiting for her. She stopped. Looking at the disserted road in despair.

'Now what?' she cried. She had nowhere to go. She had moved interstate to attend college. She had finished her course a few months ago but Roger had convinced her to put off looking for a job because they were going to get married soon. She had enjoyed the college work and after meeting Roger, she had become excited about life in the city. That feeling of excitement slowly evaporated as Roger constantly pointed out her shortcomings. He told her that she was silly to try and run her own business, let alone one that involved selling books, which was her original plan when she had left her parent's home. Even they had not been happy about her dream, they argued that books were going out-of-date with the emergence of computers, but when she had stuck to her plan, they had basically told her that she would not be welcome in their home if she failed to succeed. So, returning home and admitting that she had failed wasn't an option. Besides, she wasn't keen to return, even if she would have been welcomed. Being required to clean up after them, while they both spent most of their time drinking to excess, wasn't something she would willingly return to. Now going back to the city seemed pointless as well.

Well, right now, all she could do was to continue walking. This road must lead somewhere.

After what seemed an age, she came to a T intersection. The sign said that the city was one hundred and sixty kilometres to the left, the town they had come from was thirty-two kilometres behind her, and surprisingly, Huntersville was only six kilometres in front. It still felt strange seeing the signs in kilometres instead of miles. Hopefully there would be life, at least, in Huntersville, a place she had never heard of, although she had no idea what she would do, as she hadn't brought any money with her. Roger had said that it wouldn't be necessary. A strange idea crossed her mind, had this been his plan all along? To bring her out here in the middle of nowhere and dump her.

He hadn't been happy, three days ago, when she had told him that she thought she might be having a baby. He had told her that she needed to get rid of it, and when she had told him that she wouldn't do that, no matter what, he had stormed out of her college room. Another memory also surfaced, one that she had dismissed as being silly. The next day she had seen Roger walking across the street with his arm around a rather pretty young lady. She wasn't surprised when Roger had knocked on her door yesterday, after all that was the pattern of their relationship, they would have a fight, he would leave and the next day, he would be knocking on her door again. When she had asked him about seeing him with the other girl, he had said that he'd just met her on the sidewalk and that she told him that she was feeling unwell, so he had assisted her across the road. What Jessica now realised was that, once they had reached the other side of the road, he hadn't let go of the girl and they had disappeared into a nearby park. Now, alone on the road, her imagination told her that he was probably making another conquest. Was he really that heartless? Did he ever really love her at all?

The heat from the road below her and the sun above her was starting to make her feel quite sick. She would have to keep going. A couple of times she fell after putting her foot in a pothole, but each time she forced herself to get up, dust off her flared trousers that she had made with a borrowed sewing machine and keep going. The third time, she struggled to rise to her feet, but she didn't bother with how her trousers looked. She pushed on. By the time she reached the town of Huntersville, the sun was starting to set. She tripped again, outside what seemed to be the grandest house in Huntersville. Her involuntary cry bought a small lady, dressed in a neat straight skirt that came to just below her knee, with a plain t-shirt, to her side.

'What are you doing out here?' she asked as she helped her to her feet.

'My boyfriend dumped me beside the road more than six kilometres back, so I had to walk. Could I have a drink of water please?' He didn't even give me some money to get a train ticket back to the city.'

'Come on in, I have plenty of water and also some cream that we can put on that sunburn. I'm Susan, by the way.'

Over a couple of glasses of water and a cuppa, Jessica told Susan about how Roger had dumped her on the side of the road, and how she thought that she was carrying his baby. She told her about how they would fight, usually about something that she wanted to do, particularly if she was looking at getting a job, then he would turn up on her doorstep again, telling her that he loved her and usually she would find herself making love to him, no matter how often she had been determined not to but to wait until they had married.

'Did he ever hit you?'

'No, but he would keep at me in all sorts of ways until I gave in.'

61

Once she started to talk to Susan, she found it hard to stop, so she ended up telling her all about leaving home, her college studies, and her fears for her future.

Once she had finished, Susan was quiet for a moment.

'Is there anyone who needs to know that you are okay right now?'

'No.'

'Well, right now you need to get some sleep, let's put some cream on that sunburn and then I'll show you to the spare bedroom. Tomorrow is a new day and I'm sure that things will look better in the morning.'

Jessica was too tired and her future too bleak to argue with Susan. In that moment, Susan could have been a mass murderer waiting to kill her in her sleep and Jessica couldn't have cared less.

When she woke up the next morning it was already nearly lunchtime according to her watch. Maybe it had stopped during the night, but when she checked it again, it was still ticking.

She jumped out of bed and dressed quickly. She found Susan in the kitchen preparing lunch. She looked up as Jessica entered the room.

'Oh, you're awake.' She smiled, 'Did you sleep well?'

'Yes, I did thanks.'

'Are you hungry?'

'Actually, I am, now that you've asked.'

'Good, lunch will be ready in a few minutes.'

Over lunch they talked about the various interests that they each had. Jessica mentioned that she had no idea what she wanted to do now, since living in the city had lost its appeal. She didn't want to run the risk of seeing Roger, even by accident. Susan stopped eating and looked at Jessica.

'Yesterday, you talked about wanting to run your own business, what sort of a business would you start, if you could?'

'I love books, so I'd like to set up a bookshop or newsagency, but everyone tells me that's stupid.'

'Why?'

'Apparently, no one is going to buy books anymore. The future is all going to be about computers, apparently.'

'Not many people in country areas have computers, they are too big and expensive for most of us.'

'Ok.'

'So, in a place where there are no computers, people would still want to buy proper books, wouldn't they?' Susan smiled.

'I guess.'

'There's a newsagency here, but Mister Butler is suffering from ill health and would like to sell it. Would you be interested?'

'Oh, Susan, even if I had the experience to run a business and I don't! I don't even have enough money to buy a train ticket, let alone buy a shop.'

'How do you get experience?'

'You have to get a job, and slowly work your way up. It takes years of hard work.'

'Are you a good student?'

'I don't know.'

'What do you mean you don't know? Did you fail your course?'

'No, actually I got top marks in all my subjects.'

'So, that means you can learn.'

63

'I guess.'

'Good. Jessica, how about I get you that train ticket. Then you can go back to the city and collect your things and come back. I'd like you to give it a try for three months. If you like it, I will see to it that you get the loan to buy the newsagency.'

'Can I ask two questions first. The first one is why? You don't know me from a bar of soap. The second one is how?'

'Okay, let me answer the first one to start with. Before I came here my husband abused me, physically. I had no support from my family or his, and in the end, I tried to commit suicide. However, God had a different outcome for me. I was rescued by a farmer and his wife, who managed to get me here without anyone seeing me. Because of God's goodness to me, I promised Him that I would try and assist anyone who found themselves in a similar situation. The thing is, while Roger didn't hit you, he still abused you, and in God's eyes abuse is abuse, just like sin is sin. As I see it, God brought you to my door for a good reason. Now for the second question, after my husband and his parents were killed, I was still the heir to their estate, so I set up a trust that would enable me to help others, and there's enough in that trust to allow me to set up a loan for you to buy Mister Butler's business. There is no need for you to make up your mind straight away. Please come back. Stay for the three months and then you can decide.'

'But what if I run into Roger again, I just know that he will convince me to stay and force me to get rid of this baby.'

'What if I have someone meet you at the station? They can go with you to collect your things and even help you pack. I know a police officer in the city who can arrange for a female officer to go with you.'

'Are you sure?'

'Yes, very sure. Let me make a phone call and then we'll go and get that train ticket.'

The arrangements were made, and three days later, Jessica found herself back at Huntersville's railway station. Only this time, Susan was standing on the platform waiting to welcome her back and smiling. For the first time in her life, she had the feeling of being accepted, was this what coming home should feel like, she asked herself.

During dinner that night, Susan told Jessica that she had spoken to Mister Butler, and he was happy for her to have a couple of days to rest up and was willing to have her start work on Monday morning. 'That gives you two days, plus the weekend to get settled. We have a church service this weekend, as it's the first Sunday of the month. Most people will assume that you are another distant relative that's come to stay for a few weeks.'

'What? Do you do this a lot? Take people in just off the street.?'

'Well, yes, after my experience with my own marriage, I have always been determined to help as many people as I can. I believe that God saved me from drowning for exactly that reason.'

On Sunday, they walked to church. Jessica could see that Susan was a much-loved member of the community, and they just accepted it as very normal for Susan to bring someone new to the service.

The Reverend Smith preached but Jessica hardly heard a thing. She kept wondering what these people would think of her if they knew that she was unmarried and pregnant. After Church, they had lunch together, and she was surprised at how many people engaged her in their conversations about the drought and the price of stock as if she was just a normal member of their society. One woman, having managed to find out that Jessica was going to help Mister Butler for a while, said, 'I came here as a single mum, met my husband, and it's the best place in the world to bring up kids'. There was no judgement, Jessica knew that no-one knew she might be carrying a baby, she had listened very carefully to everything Susan said, just in case she betrayed her. Now she found herself starting to relax for the first time in weeks. She hadn't realised that she was so tense. This place was the safe haven that she had never had in her life before.

When they reached Susan's house after church, she discovered that she wasn't pregnant after all. When she told Susan, her comment was that stress often caused the body to shut down certain functions. Tears of relief flowed.

The following weeks flew by, and while Jessica found the hours long and busy, she enjoyed the work, particularly interacting with the customers, helping them to find what they wanted and catching up on the latest news from around the district. What really amazed her was the patience exercised by Mister Butler. Even on the first day, when she expressed her concerns about making mistakes, his comment to her was: 'I've never come across a mistake, yet, that cannot be fixed. Making a mistake isn't a crime, but in my eyes, trying to cover it up is. If you make one, come to me and we'll sort out how to make things right together.' Yet, each time she made a perceived mistake, he uncomplainingly went over the situation with her. When the mistake was real, he good-naturedly talked her through the various ways to correct it.

At church the next month, Reverend Smith preached about the lost sheep who had wandered off. He said that the shepherd showed patience and determination in searching for the lost sheep, and when he found it, there were no repercussions. The shepherd just carried it home, thankful that his precious sheep had been found. Reverend Smith reminded the congregation that Jesus is also very determined and patient when it comes to finding the lost members of the world. Jessica sat there thinking, *for the first time in my life, I'm not lost.*

****

'My lawyer is coming to visit tomorrow. He's going to bring the loan papers for you to sign on Monday.' They were eating dinner together on Saturday night. 'Goodness, time really does fly when you're having fun, doesn't it.'

'Are you sure that you want to do this? I'm still not convinced that I can do this on my own. It's not that I don't want to, I'm still worried that I don't have the skills yet. I can't believe that the three months is up already. How come he's coming tomorrow, it's Sunday.'

'Oh, let's just say that he enjoys coming to Huntersville. I have a feeling that, one day, he might even retire here.'

'Really?'

'Yes.'

'Will he be staying here?'

'No, he stays at the hotel when he comes out this way. Rodney always makes sure that he has a room available for him.'

'Wow.'

The next morning, as they entered the church, Susan introduced her to Mister Henderson, her lawyer, who had been speaking with Barbara, whom she knew ran a tailoring business from her flat behind the bakery.

The look on Barbara's face told Jessica that she was enjoying the conversation and was left wondering if this woman was the special attraction of Huntersville for Mister Henderson.

During the service, Reverend Smith talked about a woman at a well and how Jesus had known all about her secrets, but instead of condemning her, He invited her to take advantage of the new living water that He had to offer her. The congregation was reminded that this woman was considered by the community to be unacceptable for their social standards. This woman had five husbands, and the man she was living with when she met Jesus, wasn't even her husband. Yet, according to the Reverend, Jesus was still willing to give her the living water, which he said meant a new life in relationship with God.

'What He is saying is that it doesn't matter who you are, what you have done or where you live, He wants to have a personal relationship with you. He isn't a God that has to be worshiped in a special place or in a particular manner, He wants you to surrender your life to Him and let Him work through you where you are'. He concluded by saying, that when she discovered who Jesus was, she ran back to the village and told everyone about it. Jessica sat in the pew, thinking well, that's that then, I'm not the sort of person to be running around telling people about Jesus. He wouldn't want to be my friend.

On Monday, when all four of them were sitting down and going through the papers, Jessica still had reservations about her ability to carry out her duties on her own. In order to help her confidence, it was decided that Mister Butler would come in each evening to go over her books with her. The plan was that, as she became more confident, the visits would be extended to once a week, monthly, and after that only when she felt she needed advice. Everyone seemed to understand the damage that had been created by Roger and her parents.

****

'We're going to have a special lunch after church on Sunday,' Susan said to Jessica.

'Why, what is so special about Sunday?'

'Well, it's one year since you took over the newsagency and, therefore, a year since you became a member of our community. That's worth celebrating, isn't it?'

'I guess....'

That Sunday, Reverend Smith preached about how the world as we know it will one day come to an end. '...But, 2 Peter 3:9 says: "The Lord is not slow concerning his promise, as some count slowness; but is patient with us, not wishing that any should perish, but that all should come to repentance." God really wants all of us to be friends with Him and, just like all relationships, there will be differences in how that looks to those around us. For instance, when my wife throws me a birthday party with all my friends, there will be some who will come and they will be very excited, they will congratulate me loudly and everyone in the room will hear them, but then there are other friends who will be standing to one side, and when they get the chance, they will quietly come to me and wish me a happy birthday. There is every possibility that no-one else in the room will realise that we are friends but let me tell you, I value those friends just as much as the excited ones. They all have a part to play in my life and in supporting my work for God'.

Jessica looked up at the ceiling as she lay in her bed that night. God really wanted her to have a relationship with Him, and what was really amazing was that He was willing to accept her just as she was, just as this town had accepted her. He was willing to be her friend? Tears of relief flowed for the second time since arriving in Huntersville. 'God, I thank you that you're a patient God to all those who are afraid of the future. Please be my friend and please continue to be patient with me as I learn more about you'.

That night Jessica couldn't see into the future or the number of life-long friends that she would make. She couldn't see that she would become just as passionate as Susan and the work she was doing.

Casey

The further the train moved away from the station, the calmer her heart rate became, and she slowly stopped shaking. All she had with her was one suitcase in which she had packed the very few personal things that she just couldn't let go of. She'd left everything else behind. This had to be a clean break; she didn't want any trace of her old life to connect her to her new one.

She rubbed her arm and flinched as her hand moved over a bruise, one of the many that she had received a couple of nights before.

She had started stashing small amounts of money out of the grocery shopping after the first time Tony had hit her and the assistance from the charity for people in her position had been an absolute blessing.

Having made sure that she wore a long black skirt and top, she had covered her head with a new scarf purchased at the station first thing this morning. She wanted to look as if she was a Muslim woman. A member of the charity had collected her and her suitcase from the house and deposited her at the railway station. The lady had handed her a large envelope which contained her ticket, paperwork to change her name, and the address of a safe house where she could stay for twelve weeks without having to pay board, hopefully giving her enough time to change her name and find a job. She was also very careful to keep her head down where she was likely to encounter security cameras. She just needed to disappear into thin air.

From now on she would be known as Casey Brown. She had been told that it could take a couple of weeks for the paperwork to come through. Her greatest hope was that her husband would be too lazy to try and trace her.

After travelling all night, it was early-morning when she finally stepped onto the platform. Her legs felt a bit wobbly; she would need to find her land legs quickly or she would be drawing unwanted attention to herself. As she emerged onto the street in front of the station, she looked around. The first thing she noticed was how brown and dry the place was, there didn't seem to be a green blade of grass anywhere. Across the street there was a two-storey hotel, then a bakery, a butcher, newsagency, and a small supermarket. Next door to that was the Post Office, opposite the Police Station, and right at the end of the T-section was what looked like a small weatherboard church.

Well, at least she knew where her first port of call would be. She walked down the street to the Police Station, her legs were still shaking but her heart was determined.

As she pushed open the door, a buzzer went off, making her flinch a little. The officer behind the desk got up as she approached.

'How can I help you, madam?'

'My name is Casey Brown, however, yesterday I was Trudy Goodman fleeing an abusive situation.' She pushed up her sleeve to reveal the three bruises on her arm. 'I'm letting you know, so that if there is a missing person's report made for Trudy, she no longer exists and doesn't want to be found.'

'That's all very good Casey. Is there anything else I can do for you?' He didn't look at her but continued to type notes into the computer.

'Yes, can you tell me where I might find number ten, Church Street?'

'Yes, straight out the front door, go past the church, and the house is the third on the right.' He said without looking up from his note taking.

'Thank you.'

'You're welcome, take care now.'

The heat beat down on her and the flies were decidedly friendly as she walked past the church. There was a notice out the front announcing that services were held on the first Sunday of the month, which surprised her. The building was in need of repair, and she had assumed that it was no longer used.

The house turned out to be a small but neat Federation style home. She found herself standing in front of a long hallway as the main door was open, no doubt to let in any breeze that might be available to cool the house. Casey rang the doorbell and waited; it wasn't long before she saw a small lady making her way down the hall.

'Hello, you must be Trudy Goodman?'

'Yes, I was, but now I want to be known as Casey Brown.'

'Very good, come on in, my name is Susan and I'll show you to your room, it's down the hall towards the back of the house. The bathroom is there on the left, your room is here on the right. The kitchen is through that door and to the right, the laundry is opposite. I'll leave you to unpack and when you are ready, come and find me in the kitchen and we will have a cuppa and a chat.

Casey placed her case on the bed and noticed a care package sitting on the pillow. When she opened it, she found some toiletries, such as shampoo, conditioner, and body wash. Oh, this is nice, she thought. She had intentionally left all those things behind to give the impression that she had been spirited away. There were also some vouchers to purchase some new clothes, although she had no idea where she would get them; the town didn't seem to have any clothing stores. It wasn't long before Casey was joining Susan in the kitchen, after all, she only had what was in the suitcase to unpack.

They talked about Susan's story, which was very similar to Trudy's, but when she tried to get away there was a lot less support, giving Susan the desire to help others in the same position. The house, which enabled her to offer this help, had been left to her by her very good friend, Elsa, who had provided sanctuary when she had arrived in Huntersville many years ago.

'As far as my friends are concerned, you are a visiting niece. I've had a lot of them over the years.' She smiled at Casey.

About an hour later, Trudy returned to her room to fill out the paperwork that would allow her to change her name. As she signed her name at the bottom of the page, she realized that she would have to start calling herself by her new name every time she even thought about herself, otherwise, it would be too easy to trip herself up when she was talking to people. This was a small town, if she made a mistake then the whole town would know about it. Having completed the paperwork, she found Susan still in the kitchen and told her that she was going to post the letter and asked if there was anything that she could get for her while she was out. Susan gave her money for milk. The walk to the post office was easier this time as the air had cooled a little. She slid the envelope into the slot with a sigh. As she was turning around, she almost bumped into someone going into the building.

'Hi, you're new in town?'

'Yes, Tru... Casey Brown. I'm here visiting my aunt Susan. It seems like a nice place.' She really was going to have to stop using her old name in her head.

'Susan has a very large extended family; I was one of her nieces about ten years ago.' The lady smiled at Casey's look of surprise. 'This is a small town, honey, everyone knows everyone else's business. You can't sneeze without everyone knowing about it. I'm Jessica Blackmore, by the way. I'm sure you will find us to be a friendly lot. I own the newsagency. That's where you can find me all day every day except when we have church on the first Sunday of the month. I'm closed then. There's no point opening when there will be no customers.'

'Do you mean everyone goes to church?'

'In this place, yes, it's the only time people get together. We stay and have lunch and then I open to be available for those who only get into town once a month.'

'I've never been to church. It would probably fall down as soon as I walk in.'

'It's stronger than it looks, it's a great place to get to meet the townsfolk, besides, Susan is a pillar of our community.'

As she walked back, she started to talk to herself silently. You are a real idiot, Casey Brown! Casey, if you are not careful you are going to get caught out. Stop fooling yourself, Casey, you don't have enough in you to change your life.

Two weeks later, the bruises were healing, and she was starting to feel more relaxed. She enjoyed talking to Susan, helping her around the house and the garden. She was about to put the kettle on when Susan came in from the front yard.

'This just arrived for you.' Susan said, as she handed her a large envelope.

'Thank you.' She opened it while she was waiting for the kettle to boil. The envelope, as she suspected, contained her change of name certificate. Well, now she could get on with her new life proper. She could organise her identity documents and start looking for a job. That hadn't been possible until now, not that there was a big rush, one phone call had ensured that she received social security funds. She was keen to start doing something that would ensure true independence, but did she have enough strength to change her circumstances?

A few days later, she'd finished collecting the shopping for Susan and decided to buy a magazine to read. Having made her selection, she approached the counter; Jessica was the only person there.

'Hi, Casey. How are you doing?'

'Great thanks. The rest has worked its magic. Hey, Jessica, I don't suppose you know anywhere I could pick up some work, do you?'

'I thought you were only here on holidays.' Jessica winked at her.

'Yes, well, now that I've had a couple of weeks rest, I'm thinking of making it a working holiday.'

'What can you do?'

'I don't have a lot of experience, but I'll try anything once.'

75

'Rodney might be able to give you some cleaning work at the hotel, but there's not much going around here.'

'Okay, thanks, I'll see what happens.' She would need to talk to Susan about this, as she was still very jumpy around men. Would he be a good employer, or would she be better off moving on to somewhere else? Would she spend the rest of her life on the run?

****

It was Saturday night, and nearly a month had passed since her arrival.

'You'll come to church with me in the morning.' Susan said in such a way that it came out as a statement rather than a question.

'I've never been to church, are you sure it won't fall down?'

'God loves all his children, even those who don't acknowledge Him. I'm sure the congregation is safe; besides, it's not really going to fit the story we are telling people if you don't come.'

'Well, you could tell them I was sick.'

Susan cocked her head, 'Really? I don't think that's going to work in this town. Come, we won't bite.'

'Alright, but I don't have anything flash to wear and you'll have to tell me what to do. Like I said, I've never been to church before.'

'You don't need flash. That outfit you washed yesterday will do fine. There's no such thing as Sunday best anymore. Wait until you see what some of the farmers turn up in. God accepts us as we are, dirty and broken. All He wants to do is put us back together and make us clean.'

Sunday arrived and Casey was glad that she wasn't going to church alone. Susan introduced her, but she was still feeling very nervous as she sat down.

The minister stood up, 'Let's stand and sing the first hymn.'

Casey looked around. There were farmers in clothes that still had dirt on them, as if they had walked out of the paddock into the church. There was a teenager in torn jeans. Yeah, she knew they were the modern trend, but were they really acceptable church clothes?

After they had sung a couple of songs, the minister read from the Bible.

'I'm only going to preach on one verse this morning. The verse is 2 Corinthians 5:17 and it says this: "Therefore, if any man *be* in Christ, *he is* a new creature: old things are passed away; behold, all things are become new." What a wonderful verse this is, it tells us that when we come to Jesus and ask him to be our friend, then He will give us a new life, make us into a new creature. We can leave our old lives behind, and, with His strength, move forward, and He will help us to realise that He loves us and has made us as a person of value ....' his voice faded as her thoughts drowned him out.

A person of value, what a joke! Her only value to Tony was as a way to get into her father's business and as someone to take his frustrations and anger out on. The death of her parents, a month before she left, meant that the one restraint, fear of her father finding out, had been removed and the incidents had increased. Even here, she was a free loading guest in Susan's house. She didn't even have enough skills to get a job. What value was she to society or God?

The minister's voice cut through her thoughts. 'In Genesis 1:26, God states that man is made in His image and when He had finished, He declared that it was very good. Not just good, but very good! While that image gets dirty when we try to live our lives without Him, it gets cleaned and transformed when we come to Jesus. No-one here has done anything that God cannot forgive, it doesn't matter how useless or stupid you might think you are, God loves you and He wants you to come to Him and be reborn, remade into the best person that you can be. He is waiting for you to come, with arms opened wide, like a loving parent.'

Let's close with the hymn, *Just as I am*. Casey stood up, and each word seemed to speak directly to her. Could Jesus really make her into a new person?

Over lunch she spoke to the minister. 'Is it true that God can make you a new person. Can someone be changed that much?'

'Yes, but you have to believe in the blood of Jesus to save us from what we have done wrong.'

'But what if you're not the person doing the wrong things?'

'Everyone has done something wrong. Even just ignoring Him is wrong in the eyes of God.'

'Oh.'

'Do you want to be a new person in Christ?'

'Sir, I just want to be a new person; to start a new life.'

'God can help you with that. He is just waiting for you to step into His arms. His greatest desire is to wrap you up in them and change you from the inside out.'

That night at dinner, Casey continued the discussion with Susan. 'At church this morning, it seemed like the minister was talking directly to me, as if he knew all about me. Did you tell him my story?'

'No, absolutely not. The Holy Spirit has a special way of speaking to our hearts because He knows our secrets.'

'But how does God make me a new person? Does He change my name? Does He make me look different?'

'In my experience, when people accept Christ, they feel better about themselves and that helps them to look different. As for the new name, I think He has already taken care of that, don't you?'

'I guess.'

'Your husband made you feel worthless, God will give you the courage to try new things. When you read the Bible, you will discover that you are valuable to Him. Very valuable indeed. The best thing I found when I was starting over, was to get up each morning, read my Bible, and then, while I was having my breakfast, I would tell myself over and over whatever it was that I had learnt. I actually started with that verse Reverend Smith used this morning. I told myself over and over that I was a new creature in Christ. The other one I would recite was "I can do all things through Christ, who strengthens me." God, my dear, is where the real power to change comes from, for all of us, regardless of what we have been through. Oh, my goodness! It's starting to rain; we need that so badly.'

As Casey lay in bed that night listening to rain falling on the roof, she thought about how the rain would change the world outside, creating green pastures as it soaked into the brown dirt. Maybe, if she let the words in the Bible soak into her life, it might also change her, giving her the courage to find a job, try new things, and eventually become someone who could walk with her head held high and help others to dare to change their situation, just as Susan and Jessica were helping her. She prayed, Lord, if you're the God that doesn't change but can change me, please come into my life, and make a new person of me.

And so, her new life began, but because she couldn't see the future, she didn't know that one day, Reverend Smith would bring his new assistant to Huntersville, and she would come face to face with Tony. However, with Susan's encouragement she would listen to his apology and learn how he also found God and turned his life around. It would take a few years, but they would start again and have a new and better relationship and welcome a baby girl into their family.

Tony

Tony pulled into his driveway. The two-storey house was his pride and joy. It was on five-acres, which had been his choice because he didn't want the neighbours poking their noses into his business. Of course, he had convinced Trudy and her parents that it was an ideal block because he needed the peace and quiet away from work. The clock on the dash told him it was five in the morning. He only had time to have a shower, change his clothes and eat his breakfast before he returned to work. He had spent the night with his secretary. She had only been in his office for a couple of weeks and her slim body, cute smile, and blond hair had set his pulses racing the first time he'd laid eyes on her. Without knowing it, she had set him a challenge. He was going to make sure that she submitted to him, in the same way Trudy did. The thing was, once he had started, he had discovered that his secretary had been a very willing participant, stroking his ego on a daily basis, which had only added to the excitement of the quest. He'd never really loved Trudy, marrying her was just a means to get part of the business her father owned without having to outlay money that he didn't have. He had a moment of guilt, which had never happened before, but it didn't last long.

It was Trudy's fault that his eyes wandered, she didn't smile anymore and pulled away from him when he tried to embrace her. She couldn't cook anything that suited him and all she did all day was sit around.

He made a dash for the house; light rain making his clothes only slightly damp as he covered the distance from the car to the front door.

Entering the house, he called Trudy's name. Silence! As he walked into the bedroom, he noticed that the bed was already made. So, Trudy got up early for once, she must be in the kitchen already, so he went down to find her there. It took a while for him to register that something was wrong. Trudy wasn't cooking breakfast. Her phone, car keys, and laptop were sitting on the bench. He called her name, this time using a tone that usually brought her running.

Going back upstairs, he checked her wardrobe, there didn't seem to be anything missing. Where was she? She just couldn't disappear into thin air. Nothing. Absentmindedly he started to dial his in-laws' phone number, then stopped, they had died in a car accident only a month earlier.

As he stood there, staring at the phone in his hand, he suddenly felt defeated and deflated. Somewhere deep down inside he realised that Trudy had made her escape and the way he treated her was wrong. In a moment of clarity, he realised that he was just like his father.

He didn't dare report her missing to the police. Was it a coincidence that just yesterday, Bill had mentioned the news story about a missing woman, telling him that the police were looking at the husband as being the guilty party? His words, "They always look at the husband first and more times than not, they are right", were burnt into his brain.

He poured himself a drink, the house seemed stuffy and airless, so he went outside to the back deck.

Sitting there, he let the memories of his childhood surface. This time he saw them as an adult, watching them as if they were a film rolling in front of him. His father had treated his mother the same way he treated Trudy. His father had been his idol, he was strong, lifting large bags of grain and loading them for customers all day. He had been charming to all the customers, who seemed to think that he was a great bloke, so when he got home, he sat down and expected his wife to treat him like a king. A man's home is his castle, he would say to Tony, and my wife should treat me as such. If servants don't do as they are told then they should be encouraged to do the right thing. Tony would stand there and watch his father grab his mother by the arm, and drag her onto his lap, and say, "Isn't that right, my dear". Only this time he could see his mother's face and noticed, for the first time, that whenever his father had carried out his "encouragement" his mother had flinched and there was real fear in her eyes. The same fear that he saw in Trudy's eyes, every time he came near her. Why had that fear made him feel so much stronger than he did at work? He admitted to himself, that with the death of her parents and the way his secretary was caressing his ego, his treatment of Trudy had been even less controlled.

He took another sip and looked up at the sky. Stretching right over their backyard was the clearest rainbow that he had ever seen. As he followed the arch, he could see that each end rested in the backyards of his neighbours.

He let out an involuntary 'wow, that's beautiful!' What was it that his Sunday School teacher had told him about rainbows? Gosh, he hadn't thought about Sunday School for years. Oh yeah, Noah had built a large boat, called an ark, a long way from any water. God had told Noah to do this because the people were so bad that He was going to destroy the whole earth. Only those inside the ark would be saved. Animals had come from all around in pairs and walked into the ark. Noah had tried to get more people to find safety inside before it was too late but only his family had been saved after it had rained for forty days and nights. Eventually, the rain had stopped, and when the family and animals had left the boat, God had put a rainbow in sky as a sign that the earth would never be destroyed like that ever again. His teacher had said that Noah was a good man and that's why God had given him the job of building the ark.

In another moment of rationality, he knew that his father had been bad and so was he. God should destroy him.

He took another sip of his drink, it tasted sour, he threw what was left into the garden. As he stood up, his stomach rumbled, walking inside he put a couple of slices of bread into the toaster and switched on the jug, then decided that he would shower first.

He went upstairs and let the water flow all over him. "Are you washed by the blood of the lamb", the words from a song they had sang at Sunday School now started to run around in his head and he started to cry.

'Oh, God, I need to be washed clean. I don't deserve to be saved from the flood, but, God, please will you save me?'

That was the reason that Jesus came to earth to show how people should behave and live. Did he have the power to change his behaviour?

'*Not by yourself, you don't, but I will help you, now that you have asked.*' The statement was as clear as if someone was standing beside him, yet as he looked around to check, he found that he was the only person in the bathroom.

He dressed, ate his breakfast, and made his way back to the office. As he passed the church, which he normally didn't give a second glance at, the notice on the sign out the front stood out. **"Be strong and courageous; do not be frightened and do not be dismayed, for the Lord your God is with you wherever you go." Joshua 1:9.**

He pulled over, staring at the sign. Changing his life was going to take courage, yet here was a sign that was telling him that God would help him. He needed to start by ending the relationship with his secretary. What he did after that, he had no idea. 'God, please lead me and give me strength to follow'. He restarted the car and drove to work.

As he walked past his secretary's desk, she looked up, 'You're late.'

'I know, please come into my office.' She smiled, picked up her notebook and followed him.

He sat down, and as she made a move to come around to his side of the desk, he pointed to the chair opposite.

'Please take a seat, I need to say something very important.' She frowned but did as she was asked. Tony breathed a prayer; 'God, help me to do this right'.

'I want to apologise to you. I have treated you badly. I have not respected you in the way that I should have. I'm sorry, you deserve better.'

'But...'

'No buts, I'm a married man, and not only have I treated you badly, but also my wife. I need to change my behaviour and it starts right here. If you want to transfer to another department, I'll be happy to make sure that happens for you.'

'What bought this on, did your wife find out?' her laugh had a nasty edge to it.

'No, my wife has no knowledge of our relationship, and she may never know about it.'

'Well, what's the harm then?'

'Oh, God, please help me fight this temptation'.

'The harm is that I'm damaged goods and if we continue, it will destroy all your future relationships. Which department would you like to be transferred to?'

'You don't look very damaged to me,' she used her most charming tone.

'The most extreme damage can't be seen on the outside.'

'It's probably best if I just resign and find work somewhere else. I still think we could have been good together.' She walked out of the room with a very pronounced swagger that Tony knew was a deliberate attempt to get him to relent.

That night he went over the day, amazed at how, once Sandy had walked out, he had found a new secretary from the clerical section within minutes. How, when a customer rang, he managed to stop himself from telling them that the order was on the way, when in fact it hadn't even been looked at. He had told them that due to a backlog in orders it would be a couple of weeks before their order could be shipped, and if they wanted to take their business elsewhere, he understood. The customer had thanked him for being honest with them and that they would continue to do business with them. The surprise on the head of Shipping's face when Tony had visited his office and asked what could be done to help the department to catch up instead of tearing strips off him for being behind gave him a very good feeling, something he had never felt before. He'd lost count of the number of people who did a "double take" because he had smiled at them when he walked by. He thanked God for helping through his first day of his new existence, and asked for courage to continue, hoping His power would change the rest of his life.

'Just take one day at a time, and when you fall down, I'll help you get up and start again.' The voice that he had heard in the bathroom that morning was back.

'What about Trudy, would he ever be able to make it up to her?'

'Let's just work on you right now, Trudy is safe. You both need to heal through my power to change before either of you can move forward.'

****

Tony woke, it was Sunday morning, he moved and groaned, his body hurt in places that he didn't know existed. No gym workout, ever, had produced this much pain. He'd managed to get through the first week of his new life. There had been challenges, like the time he'd snapped at a trainee, he'd watched the poor fellow walk across his office with slumped shoulders. Was it his imagination or did Tony hear him mutter, 'Be strong and courageous; do not be frightened and do not be dismayed, for the Lord your God is with you wherever you go'? As he'd reached the door, he'd lifted his head, squared his shoulders, and as his hand was about to turn the handle Tony realised what he had done.

'STOP.' The trainee, paused and turned to face him, 'I'm sorry, that wasn't called for. Please come back and sit down and let's go over this again.'

Over the next hour, Tony had listened to his approach to the problem and discovered that the young man really had a much better understanding of the situation than he did himself.

Yesterday had also been a challenge. He'd got up, eaten breakfast out on the deck wondering what he was going to do with himself. They rarely spent time at home over the weekends, if they did, he always insisted on having friends over for drinks or a meal. Tony wanted to be seen either at parties or in public places, making it look as if they were the perfect couple enjoying the best things in life. As he placed his things on the sink, he noticed the dirty dishes. A whole week's worth. 'Oh, these stink!'

'*It's time for you to do the cleaning yourself.*' There was that voice again, and as he looked around, and noticed the dirty benches and floors, the rubbish on the table.

'Oh dear. I guess Trudy didn't sit around all day.' He walked into the bedroom, yes, he'd managed to make the bed, but there on the bathroom floor, were his discarded clothes. 'How do I clean this up?'

'*Google.*'

So, for the rest of the day, he'd Googled; how to use their washing machine, how to wash and vacuum floors, he'd packed the dishwasher and had to do the dishes twice to make sure they were really clean. At morning tea, he'd discovered that all the milk was gone. He'd survived the week by eating "Take-out", but he was sick of the same thing each night. At the supermarket, while getting milk, he discovered ready-made, microwaveable meals. At least this was better than hamburgers and chips. Taking his meal outside, he looked at the lawn, it was starting to look a bit long. Trudy must have done that as well during the week. He'd never considered the amount of work that it took to keep their home the way he wanted it. He went in search of the mower, again, he googled how to start this monster of a machine. By the time he'd finished, it was just starting to get dark. Thank goodness, that must be all the jobs done now, but as he walked back to the house, he noticed the washing still hanging on the clothesline. What! You've got to be kidding, I'm so tired. He pulled the clothes off the line, dragged himself into the house, dumped the basket on the couch, and pulled himself up the stairs to bed. He was so tired he couldn't be bothered eating.

Tony looked at the clock. It was mid-morning. Well, there were jobs still to be done. That washing wasn't going to fold itself. Going downstairs, he started to get his breakfast, looking around he expected the kitchen to look clean, after all he'd cleaned it up yesterday. However, what met him was the dirty dishes from his lunch, numerous coffee mugs and even a couple of glasses, the benches were covered in spilt coffee and milk.

'Really, how does one person make so much mess?'

He ate his breakfast outside again, this time more because he felt so discouraged by how much work needed to be done inside, at least his garden would look clean but even that didn't look as good as it usually did. He really had been blind.

After his brunch, he just needed to get away from the mess. He got in his car and drove down the street, again, he stopped outside the church. There was another notice that he hadn't seen before announcing that there would be a service that evening. He decided that he needed to attend.

He went home, tackled the kitchen, hung his clothes, and had an early evening meal. Then he showered, dressed, and went to church.

The preacher talked about how God wanted people to know that He loved them and the best way for that to happen was for us, His people, to live, work, and behave in the same manner that Jesus had when He had lived on earth. At the end of the service everyone was invited to stay for a cup of tea or coffee and fellowship in the hall. Tony had no intention of staying but on reaching the door, Reverend Jones introduced himself.

'I'm Reverend Jones, is this your first time with us?'

'Tony Goodman, yes, it is. That was interesting.'

'Goodman, hey. Do you live up to your name?' The preacher smiled at his joke.

'Actually, I don't' and he was embarrassed to feel tears forming. The man looked at him in sympathy, 'How about we talk in my office.' He spoke quietly to a woman and led Tony to a room with comfortable chairs off to the side of the hall. They were only talking for a few minutes when there was a quiet knock at the door, the same lady entered with a tray containing two cups of coffee, a mug of tea and some biscuits. 'This is my wife'

How do you do? I wasn't sure if you would prefer tea or coffee so take what you want, and I'll leave you in peace.' He found this man so easy to talk to and found himself telling him that He had very recently felt God's forgiveness for a life that was less than charming. He didn't go into details and the Reverend didn't press him.

'The most important thing now is to put your past behind you and look forward. We have small group meeting on Wednesday nights, so people can study the Bible and find out how God really wants them to live. They are held here at the church, and you are most welcome to come.'

As he lay in bed that night, he thought about what the preacher had said, and prayed, 'Lord, how come you're so patient with me?'

'That is what love is and I have big plans for you.'

Little did he know how big. There would be years of learning how to deal with his anger, followed by more years of Bible College and eventually he would take a position as Reverend Smith's assistant in the lead up to his retirement as pastor of his church and the many congregations on his circuit. The biggest part of the plan was when they attended the small congregation of Huntersville, he would come face to face with Trudy, known now as Casey Brown. With the help of Reverend Smith, they would come to know each other again and eventually fall in love properly and start a new life together.

Reverend Smith

Reverend Smith was driving slower than he normally did. He was enjoying the company of his companion, the Reverend Anthony Goodman, and as they had left earlier than usual this morning, there wasn't the need to rush. Having company was such a rare event and he planned to make the most of it.

His doctor had advised him to slow down, or his life would be over due to his failing health. After a long discussion with his wife, they had decided that, if someone would be willing to assist him, he would be able to continue working for a few more years. She understood his emotional and spiritual ties to all the people he had cared for during his working life as a pastor. It was hoped that whoever came to assist him, would, over that few years, come to love his people as much as he did and take over full-time, making the transition smoother for all concerned.

Each time Anthony accompanied him, he would tell him everything that he could about the community during the drive, but this was his first trip to Huntersville. Huntersville was a unique community; it always had been particularly special to Reverend Smith.

'The first duty that I carried out in Huntersville was to bury a farmer. He'd died a month after a farming accident. I guess every first event is imprinted on your mind more than others, but I remember that one because of the strength shown by the man's wife, Elsa. When I visited her just before the funeral, I discovered that she had been running the farm all by herself since his accident. I asked her what she would do now, and her reply was "I'll get on by myself and God will send me help when I need it." Her only family was a sister who was unable to attend because she lived so far away. When I asked if she was disappointed, she told me that her sister probably hadn't even received the news yet, the mail was pretty slow back then, but she was sure that she would come as soon as she could. Over the years, I watched that woman take care of a lady by the name of Susan, who had been treated so badly by her husband that she had tried to drown herself in a river. Months later, she also had an accident, she sold the farm and brought the bakery and a house in town and continued to work in the shop front, while Susan worked the long hours in the back of the shop. I performed her marriage, buried her second husband, and laid her to rest as well. Susan found her. She was in her favourite chair reading her Bible. She always got up at four thirty and read her Bible. One day I asked her why she got up so early even after she moved to town. She told me that it was a habit from her days on the farm. "Pastor", she said, "It's the only spare time I could find while we were farming and if I didn't listen to the good Lord first thing in the morning, the rest of the day was a bit wonky, and I spent most of the day wondering what I'd missed". I asked if that was what happened the day of her accident and she said, "No, Pastor, that was just God's way of telling this stubborn heart it was time to sell. My Bible verse that morning was John 10:4."'

'And when he putteth forth his own sheep, he goeth before them, and the sheep follow him: for they know his voice, that was the verse God gave me the morning the college chaplain told us about your request for an assistant. What happened to Susan?'

Oh, she is the treasure of Huntersville. I remember the sermon I preached the first Sunday she attended church. I was led to preach on Hebrews 10:11-14. I remember saying that, while churches tell us that committing suicide was an unforgiveable sin because you wouldn't have a chance to repent, I believe that God tells us here that He has already forgiven us in advance. I didn't know why I was meant to say that and many of my parishioners questioned me after church which is another reason why I remember it so well. Weeks later, she told me about her almost drowning and how she had really wanted to die and how that passage had helped her to let go of her guilt over it. When her husband and his parents were killed in a car accident, she came into a sizeable inheritance that enabled her to set up a trust to help others who found themselves in difficult circumstances, Elsa then left her the house she had purchased when she sold the farm. They are known as her extended family. She said it was fitting that the money be used for the good of others, even though her real family had caused so much pain. Barbara was the first one I remember. Her son and his wife considered her to be their personal slave and almost starved her to death. When she arrived in Huntersville, she was literally skin and bone, eventually, she healed, set up a tailoring business, and when the solicitor who helped Susan set up the trust took early retirement, she married him, and they faithfully attend our monthly services.'

'Do all the members of Susan's extended family remarry?'

'No, not all of them. She has helped so many people, many of them have stayed just long enough to heal and find the courage to move on, only a few have stayed for good. Jessica has never married, her story isn't as sad as some, but she stayed in town and owns the newsagency. She's a very quiet person, she never made a public declaration of her faith but I'm very certain that her relationship with Jesus is on firm ground these days. It took her a long time to come to that point though. The other person that stayed was Casey Brown. She's about your age and set up a gift shop, with the help of the trust. She sells all sorts of things, plants, knitting, pottery, craft supplies, and locally grown vegies. The only thing she doesn't sell is books, new or second-hand, she was determined not to tread on Jessica's toes. They are very good friends. Well, here we are. Time to meet your new flock.'

Reverend Smith was introducing Anthony to each member of the congregation. There were several farming families being introduced and Anthony whispered, 'how on earth am I going to ever remember all their names?' He was shaking hands as he was introduced, 'Barbara and Gary Henderson'

'Ah, I've heard about your work on the way out here, nice to meet you.'

'Jessica Blackmore.'

'Now you're the lady who runs the newsagency. It's nice to be able to put a face to a name.'

'Susan Landtry.'

'Now, I understand that you are the treasure of Huntersville.'

'Well, that's probably true if a treasure is considered an antique.' she replied with a smile.

'Cas...'

'Trudy!' Reverend Smith watched Casey's face turn white as a sheet.

'No. It can't be!' She started shaking and turned to Susan, 'I can't stay, I'm going home. She turned and ran.

'No, Wait.' Anthony made to go after her. Susan reached out, placing her hand on his arm.

'Leave it for now. I take it you're her husband?' Susan queried.

Yes, I was when she was Trudy Goodman. I didn't know she was living here. I know you may not believe me, but God has been working very hard on me since she left. I've been praying for her for so many years and for a chance to tell her how sorry I am for the way I treated her. Oh, goodness, I don't think I can lead the service this morning.'

'It's okay, I'll go and make sure she is alright. Young man, it's time to show us what you are really made of. You carry on here, have lunch with the congregation, and then it might be an idea for you to come to my place for a cuppa before you head to Harrisvale. I should be able to tell you how she is. Hopefully, Casey will join us, if she doesn't, then you are just going to have to keep praying for the time being.' With that, Susan walked down the street in Casey's wake.

Three hours later, Reverend Smith and Anthony walked into Susan's kitchen, where an afternoon tea of biscuits, tea, and coffee was almost ready for them. The formal dining room had been turned into a bedroom, first for Elsa and then Susan, years ago, this enabled them to have room to allow some people to stay. They were never able to have more than two people staying at one time and currently there were no guests.

Casey was sitting in a chair, her elbows on the table and arms crossed against her chest, looking pretty distressed. Anthony sat down opposite her. Susan and Reverend Smith stood side by side at the sink and quietly watched.

'I'm so sorry. I really didn't know you were here. I've been praying for you for so many years. I wanted a chance to tell you that I am sorry for the way I treated you and to thank you for walking out on me. If you hadn't, I may never have found my way to God. He told me that you were safe but not where you were or that you had changed your name.' Casey looked up, watching him, it seemed that she was trying to work out if he was being truthful. 'I don't expect you to believe me, but I believe that God has led me here as assistant pastor for this circuit, so that I could tell you how sorry I am. Now that I have found you, I'd like the chance for us to get to know each other again, even if it's just as friends. All I asked God for, was the chance to say I was sorry, and today, he has answered that prayer.'

Reverend Smith felt Susan make a move beside him. 'Let's have that cuppa.'

There was some activity as the electric jug was boiled and carried to the table, coffees and teas made and handed around. Casey didn't move.

'How did lunch go?' Susan asked.

'Everyone wanted to know if Casey was alright. In the end I had to make a public announcement that she wasn't feeling well. Mister Blackman stopped lunch and made us take time out to pray for you.' Reverend Smith said as he looked at Casey, 'You are very special to this community. You know that, don't you?' Casey nodded but didn't smile.

'I think it was Missus Robertson, that was sitting across from me at the table, that said, "I remember when Casey came to town, I didn't see any bruises, but she had the look of a battered wife about her, *and if you hurt her*, it will be very easy for us to help you understand how painful that was for her"'.

'What did you say?' Susan asked.

'What could I say, I just told her that I would keep that in mind.'

'The only person that knew was Susan.' Casey said, fear returning to her eyes.

'It wouldn't have mattered if you had told the whole town. I deserve everything that is due to me.' At which time Reverend Smith noticed that Casey relaxed a little.

'So, tell us the story of how God found you.' Susan asked. Reverend Smith noticed that he took responsibility for his crimes. Not once did he blame Casey or anyone else for that matter.

He started at the point where he had come home in the morning to find that the house was empty, he even confessed about having spent the night with his secretary and how the rainbow had appeared while he was having a drink on the deck, and he'd remembered some of the things that he had been taught at Sunday School. Susan and the Reverend laughed when he told them about his first weekend of cleaning up after himself, even Casey smiled slightly, when he said that he'd never felt so sore, and that it was harder than any gym workout. He looked at Casey and his voice quavered, "I don't know how you did it. You even managed to keep the house and garden organised when your arm was broken.

She sobbed, 'Painfully, I had been hurting for so long that I'd forgotten what it was to not be in pain until I'd been here for a month, besides, I wouldn't have been game to not do it. That first Sunday when we were going to church, I woke up, rolled over and thought, wow, nothing hurts for once.'

'Oh, Trudy, I'm so sorry.' Anthony looked very miserable. 'I can't believe that I accused you of not doing anything all day. What I have come to realise is that, if the housework is done properly, it looks as if nothing has been done, but to achieve that, someone has to work their butt off all the time.'

'Look, there's one thing that you are going to have to get used to, and I'm sorry, but this is going to be not negotiable and that is, my name is now Casey. I've lived here for years under that name, and everyone knows me by it. It's also my official name according to my "change of name" certificate. You're going to have to start thinking of me as Casey in your head, if you want any chance of moving forward, that's what I had to do'.

Anthony nodded, 'Fair enough, it might take me awhile though.' He took a swig of his tea. 'Over time, I realised that I had learnt that behaviour from my father but that it was my obligation to unlearn it. Like an alcoholic, I have to take it one day at a time, and sadly, I can't promise that I will never fall back into those bad behaviours, which is why I don't really expect us to be able to resume our married relationship.'

'As far as God is concerned you are both still married.' Reverend Smith said thoughtfully, 'how that works for the government authorities I don't really know.'

'Casey could continue to use her new name; many married couples do these days.' Susan said thoughtfully.

If Tru, oh I mean, Casey, ever decides that she wants to resume our relationship, I would like to have a recommitment ceremony. This time I won't be asking Casey, see I can do it, to obey me. This time around we will be equal partners.'

'But the Bible says that a wife should submit to her husband, and someone has to be the head of a family.'

'No way, and please don't freak out, I'm really not trying to push you into anything here, but any future relationship has to be an equal relationship. I can't afford to give myself even a smidgen of that power again. I cannot risk opening the door that might allow me to fall back into the habit of thinking of her as a possession, someone to be controlled. I cannot, will not, go there again.'

'What happens when you can't agree on a major decision, such as a move to another congregation.'

'I've prayed about that, and if that situation ever arises, we will be sitting down and talking about what a move would mean for each of us and work out what the pros and cons would be. However, I've already decided that, until the Holy Spirit tells both of us separately that the move is a good thing, I stay where I am.'

'You've thought about this a lot, I take it?' Casey looked amazed.

'Yes, and prayed about it every day as well. In fact, it's just occurred to me that, if you were to continue using your new name, it might make it easier for me to remember that you are my equal, and someone that I should honour, because I now know that is what God wants me to do. Look Tr..., Casey, I'm not going to rush you on this. We need to take our time; we really didn't know each other, even when we were living as husband and wife. We are both very different people now... *You* need to know if this is what God wants you to do. If you decide that's it's not, then I still would like to be friends. I'm leaving this in God's hands. He knows what I want, but if it's not in His plan then I'm happy to continue working for Him on my own.'

'I agree that we don't really know each other, and I will see what God wants me to do, but at this point I'm unwilling to make any promises.'

'Fair enough. Thank you for hearing me out though.'

It was time for them to leave, as they now only had just enough time to make it to Harrisvale for their evening service.

That night, Reverend Smith climbed into bed absolutely exhausted. Sundays were always tiring but today's drama had brought on an extra weariness. However, sleep evaded him for a while as he went over the day's events at Huntersville. He thought about Casey and Anthony, both these people had been dear to his heart even before he knew that they had been married in their past lives and wondered what their future would hold, but as he closed his eyes he prayed, God I'm so glad that you're the God of new beginnings.

He wasn't to know that eventually they would be joined again, as husband and wife, working alongside each other for the Lord. Right then, he never dreamt that after the death of Susan Landtry, Casey would have a successful pregnancy and give birth to a daughter, whom they would name Susan to honour the woman who had been such a large part of their recovery and new life together.

Sargent

Sargent Morgan walked cautiously into the reception room of the hotel. He only half listened to the speeches that were being given by the senior members of the force. He didn't come to the city very often, only if work necessitated it, or in this case, the retirement dinner of Inspector Davis.

He still thought of him as Sargent Davis. He'd been his immediate supervisor when his wife and baby son had been killed by a drunk driver. Six months after the accident, Sargent Davis had requested an interview. He still remembered that interview word for word.

"How you doing, son?"

"Sarg, I'm doing okay"

"Really? This has been a tough time for you and there's no shame in admitting that things are still rough going."

"Well, to be honest with you, I'm finding the city a bit claustrophobic. I mean, all you ever get to see happen here is the same old roundabout. The crooks do the wrong thing, we book them, lock them up, the judges let them out, they go out and commit another crime and we're right back where we started. It seems a bit hopeless to me at the moment, but I'll get there eventually."

"Well, you're a good officer and I think it might be helpful for you if you had a change of scenery. Do you think that might help?"

"Depends, I guess."

"Well, I know that there's a position coming up in Huntersville."

'Huntersville, where on earth is that?'

'In the middle of nowhere, Sargent Davis had smiled. The thing is Huntersville is a small town, but it serves a very large rural community and it's a very special place to me.'

'What makes it so special?'

'One resident, by the name of Susan Landtry, helps people who find themselves living in difficult circumstances. She gives them assistance through a trust that she set up. So, the town needs someone with our authority to step in when necessary. But.. The reason I think this move would be good for you is that you also get to see the good side of her work. Think about it over the weekend, and if you would like to apply for it, come and see me next week.'

He'd had that weekend off and spent the whole time feeling like a caged lion. On the Monday morning he'd seen Sargent Davis and he had told him in more detail why Huntersville was special to him. His application had been accepted and a month later he had found himself installed in the station house there. Acceptance by the community, the wide-open spaces around the town, and time, had allowed his heart to finally heal. He'd been there for about three years when he had fallen in love with a local farmer's daughter and married her. They now had two children, a boy, and a girl who would be starting school next year. He liked the Inspector a lot, which was a good thing, considering that he was, in fact, moving to Huntersville to live his retirement out.

It felt kinda fitting that the Inspector was retiring next week, because it would allow him one final duty, that Sargent Morgan knew he would really want to carry out. He looked up as the man in question stood up to speak.

'Fellow officers, I thank you for all the kind words that have been said about me here tonight and I am proud of the team of officers that will continue to head up our Domestic Violence Unit after I leave, but it wouldn't be as good as it is today if it wasn't for the courage of one woman, by the of name Susan Joanne Landtry. I had a phone call this morning notifying me that she also has entered into her final retirement. It will be my greatest honour to speak at her second funeral as my final duty. Very few of you are old enough to remember a time when domestic violence wasn't even allowed to be recognised by us. You see, when I started out, the police were not allowed to interfere between a man and his wife. Susan's husband was one man who made no secret of his contempt for his wife. I knew that it wouldn't be long before she ended up in the graveyard, which she did after her home burnt down. I vowed that day, that I would do what I could to assist, not just women, but men as well, who wanted help to break out of such miserable circumstances.

Yes, in the beginning I bent the law but not to breaking point, and I'm proud to say, because of her work, we now have a much better understanding and treatment for those in difficult circumstances. I know you are wondering how it is that she will be having a second funeral. Months later, when it was safe, she resurfaced. She'd been rescued by a farming couple after a failed drowning attempt and had been living in a small town in the middle of nowhere. She set up a trust that enabled her, and our unit, to carry out many rescues. It was her life-long work and it's been a privilege to know and work alongside her. I heard words like courage and persistence mentioned a lot particularly in regards to my efforts, yet I'd rather you honour the woman who made much of our work possible. So, please raise your glasses to a woman who worked much harder than I ever did to make this world a better place. Susan Joanne Landtry, may she finally rest in peace.'

'Susan Joanne Landtry.' The whole room said with one voice and without a formal request, the room fell silent for a whole minute.

Once people started to talk and move about again, Sargent Morgan noticed the Inspector walking towards him.

'Nice to see you here. How are things going out there?'

'Not bad, I have to thank you for encouraging me to move there. You were right, the change of scenery has given my life a lot more purpose and meaning.'

'That's good, I knew you were a good fit for that place. How's the wife and kids?'

They're great, Mandy goes to school next year. They grow up way too fast. Harry is doing very well. Karen was worried that he would have trouble settling in, but it seems to be working out okay. We've just got to help him see that his schoolwork relates to life.'

'Well, that's good, I look forward to catching up with you next week. I'll be out a couple of days before the funeral. Jane's looking forward to finally seeing the house finished.'

'It's looking good, the men started the landscaping yesterday, so, it really should be finished by the time you arrive.'

****

Inspector Davis and his wife drove down the street to be met with a sight they had never ever seen before.

'What the hell? What is going on?' Jane said, her voice a mixture of surprise and concern.

'I have no idea. I'm sorry, honey I know you wanted to see the house first, but I think we'd better call in at the station and see Morgan before we head out there.'

'That's fine, I don't understand what all these people are doing. Is this what Bethlehem was like on that first Christmas? This is unreal, you have a job to move, there are so many people.'

They pulled up outside the police station, and looked in dismay at the line of people standing outside waiting to get in.

'I think we'll go around the back to the residence. I've a feeling there's work to be done.'

'I think you are right. This is unbelievable.' The inspector started the car, drove around the block, and knocked on the back door of the house.

Karen met them at the door. 'Oh, thank goodness you are here. Gerry could use a hand I think, but I'll make you a cuppa first, come on in.'

'What is going on?'

'All these people have turned up for Susan's funeral. The place is packed out, there are SUV's camping at the showground, in the park, and out along the roads into town. Gerry is trying to get hold of temporary toilet facilities and keeps getting questions about the funeral that he has no answers to. All these people won't fit in the church.'

'Okay, I'll take that tea with me, give me one for Gerry and I'll see what I can do.'

Inspector Davis walked into the front office, carrying a mug in each hand. He placed them on the table, opened a cupboard, and pulled out a bullhorn that was sitting on the shelf.

He raised it. 'Ladies and gentlemen, please make your way outside. As soon as we have met with a few people we will tell you what arrangements have been made and we will make a public announcement in two hours outside in the street. Now, please exit this building.' There was some grumbling, but the room was emptied in no time at all.

'Phew! Thank you. I never expected this many people to show up for Susan's funeral. I knew she helped a lot of people, but this beggars belief.'

'I understand, here have a cuppa. Have you contacted Reverend Smith and Anthony Goodman?'

'Yes, they are both on their way here. I rang them last night because I could see then that there was going to be too many people to fit into the church. They should be here any minute.'

'How about you ring one of their mobile phones and tell them to come around to the house. That way they won't be mobbed as well.'

'Good idea'. Morgan picked up the phone, dialled a number, which was answered very quickly, he gave the instructions and hung up.

'They'd just reached the edge of town and were staggered by what they were seeing as well. That will be their car now.'

'Right, can we use your sitting room? There's a bit more room there and it's way more comfortable, and the ladies can also be part of the discussions, because I think we are going to need some lateral thinking here.'

'Yeah, no problem. Karen took the kids out to the farm this morning so they wouldn't get in the way, and besides, it's probably safer for them out there at the moment.'

'Right! Now, let's see what we can do.'

The two Reverends, two Police Officers, and four wives sat down and sipped their tea before anyone said anything.

'Well, the church isn't going to hold all these people, we'll need the speaker system from Harrisvale, we can bring it with us tomorrow but where else can we have the service?'

'The only place with enough room would be the showground. I'll ring Jessica and see if there will be any problems. They are not predicting any rain over the next week.' Casey took her mobile out of her bag, stood up, moved to the kitchen, and returned a few minutes later with the good news that Jessica thought that using the showground was a good idea. 'She'd come over and help except, she is swamped with customers over there.'

'Alright, the other big problem is toilet facilities.' Gerry said. 'I can get some over from the Harrisvale, but we'll need a truck driver to go over and drive it back, otherwise they can't deliver until the day after tomorrow.'

'Rodney, from the Hotel, has a truck licence. If Karen and I can man the front desk of the hotel for him, I think he would be willing to help out.' Casey got up and headed to the kitchen again. Returning a few minutes later, she looked at Karen and smiled. 'We're up. Rodney wants to get some more drink supplies anyway, so he was pleased when I suggested we help out for a few hours to allow him to get away. I'll go over and you come over when you're ready. He said that it should only take him three hours.' She walked over, kissed Anthony on the cheek, collected her handbag, and left the room.

'I'll give it to Casey, she has great organisational skills, wonderful powers of persuasion, and unlimited energy when it comes convincing people to pitch in when it's necessary.' Reverend Smith said as Karen also stood up and went to get changed.

'I never really appreciated how good her skills were until she had the courage to walk out on me. What a lot of time I wasted through my selfishness.'

'Now, Anthony, there's no need to go back down that road, God has worked a miracle in your life and Casey's, and you need to continue to look forward not backwards. Taking things slowly with Casey was the very best way to grow together and find true love, don't destroy your new life together by dwelling on the past. Remember what Proverbs 17:9 says.'

"Love prospers when a fault is forgiven, but dwelling on it separates close friends." They quoted together.

'Gentlemen, we need things organised so we can make that public announcement. We can use the speakers on the police car.'

'Well, at least now we can tell the masses that the funeral will be held at the showground, and that the toilets are on the way. I guess the other thing that needs to happen is to enlist the help of as many people as we can to assist with the heavy lifting. We are going to need some sort of seating, because the grandstand isn't useable, there are the pews out of the church but if they were going to be enough, we'd been able to hold it in the church.' Reverend Smith looked thoughtful.

'I think Karen's dad might be able to bring some bales of hay in for people to sit on. Inspector, I'm so glad that you decided to come out early, it's been a great help having you here.'

'Right, well our two hours is nearly up, so let's get out there and get this show on the road.' The inspector stood up.

'Inspector would you mind taking the lead on this, I know it's my station but honestly, I'm exhausted.'

'It's all good, lad. I'm going to be a member of this community from now on anyway, so I'm happy to help out.'

****

For two days everyone worked hard. Volunteer visitors and locals alike were determined to make sure that Susan had a great send off. The day of her funeral promised to be warm and sunny.

The showground was packed, people sat on bales and camping chairs while others spread out blankets on the ground. They say that necessity is the mother of invention, and many hands make light work. Both statements were definitely proved to be correct on this occasion.

When it was his turn to speak, Inspector Davis stood up and looked at the crowd. During the last couple of days, he'd had a chance to speak to many of these people. He was amazed to discover that each and every one of them had been helped through Susan's work or knew of someone who had been.

'Ladies and Gentlemen, Susan would be absolutely staggered to discover that she had helped this many people. I first met Susan when I was a lowly constable. Her husband made no secret of his disdain for her. In those days, we were unable to intervene between husband and wife, and I was certain that Susan would end up in the graveyard sooner rather than later. Then one day, her house burnt down, and she disappeared. I made a vow that day that I would do everything in my power to assist those who found themselves in similar circumstances. It was assumed that she'd perished in that fire and a funeral was held for her, on those grounds. So, today is actually her second funeral. After her husband and his parents died in a car accident, Mister Henderson was able to find her, and discovered that she had been taken in, protected and loved by this community. It was at that time that she was able to set up a trust fund, using her late husband's estate, to help those in similar circumstances. She always considered it important to do something good with it, in order to balance out the pain the family had caused.

One problem she knew would be difficult to solve was how to hide people while they were being whisked away. That was how we came up the idea of the "Trust Box". Yes, we had the box made, but back then it had airholes in the sides and lid.' He pointed to the box at the front of the crowd. 'The first time it was used, a mother, who was being slowly starved by her children, slept in the box all night while the train carried her out here. Over the years there have been many others who have been saved through this and many other means. With the improvements of assistance for victims we eventually retired the Trust Box.

Susan must have known that her time was coming to an end, because when I spoke to her on the phone just two weeks ago, she told me that the Trust Box was being brought out of retirement for one last time. She had arranged for it to be fixed up to meet coffin regulations. She said, "Inspector, I can't think of a more suitable use for it than to let me rest in it until my Lord returns and I go to meet Him in the sky."

Ladies and Gentlemen, it has been my privilege and honour to work alongside this very courageous woman, and the work she did. She didn't just talk about helping others, she worked first and talked later. Over the years, and I have known her for more than I am willing to admit, she made representations to anyone and everyone whom she thought might be able to do something to help prevent the increasing incidents of Domestic Violence.

I know that every one of you will continue to honour her memory by continuing to make sure that every human being is treated with respect and taking care of those who are struggling to take care of themselves. Now, to close this service, I'm going to get Jessica to come up and read a poem that she found in Susan's Bible marking the passage that was read earlier. Thank you, Jessica.' He sat down and listened as Jessica stood up and read:

> You're healing to those in pain.
> You're peace to those in chaos.
> You're calm for those who stress.
> You're persevering with those who are slow.

You're determined with those who destroy.
You're mercy to those in depravity.
You're love to those who are hated.
You're strength to those who are weak.
You're courage to those who fear.
You're light in the darkness.
You're able to see all of us.
You're always beside us
You're everything to us,
Lord, you're eternal life to those who rest in You.

And the whole crowd said, 'Amen'.

Other Books by this Author

All these books, with the exception of *Whispers from on High*, are available as eBooks

Turning Water into Wine
100 Stories of God's Hand in Life

More Water into Wine
100 Stories of God's Hand in Life

Still More Water into Wine
100 Stories of God's Hand in Life

Reflections
Australian Stories from my Father's Past

365 Glasses of Wine
Short Devotionals for each day of the year

Conversations with Myself – Volume 1
100 Stories of Hope, Faith, and Determination

Whispers from on High
Poems and short stories

Fireside Stories – With Wendy Brown
Australian Family Tales

Christmas Journeys – A Trilogy
3 Stories of Love and Family, spanning across the decades.

Like Father… Like Son
A story of Family, betrayal, and ultimately forgiveness

Follow Helen Brown on:
Facebook: https://www.facebook.com/HelenBrownCollection/

Instagram: https://www.instagram.com/helen_brown_books/

Pinterest: https://www.pinterest.com.au/helenbrown58726/

Connect with Reading Stones for other great reads:
https://www.facebook.com/Reading-Stones-Publishing-and-Editing-Services-252366958298920